"Sarah, go home while I can still let you go," Asa said. **"This can't work. I'd make you miserable."**

"Why don't you let me decide?"

"I'm compulsively neat," he went on, as if trying to convince himself as well as Sarah. "My bathroom doesn't have any extra toothbrushes because I don't like people in my house. My truck sits too high off the ground for a lady to climb in and out of because I don't welcome a woman's company. In other words, I'm a man who has a plan for every part of his life, and you're a lady—"

"Without one," she finished. "Maybe you're right. But I think there are times when it's better to forget all your plans and fly blind into the sun."

She couldn't read the expression in his eyes in the darkness, but she could feel the tension in his touch. He should have loosened his grip if he wanted her to believe he was pulling away, instead of moving a little closer.

"Asa, I'm not very smart about men, and I'm not even being honest about why I'm here. The real reason I came"—her voice dropped into a throaty whisper—"is because I think I want you."

She felt the erratic beat of her heart and sensed that his was echoing hers. A long moment passed before he spoke.

"Are you sure you want to take a chance getting involved with a man like me?"

Sarah closed her eyes and tried to think logically. "Do I want to get involved with you? I already am." She was rewarded with a groan of desperation as his arms locked around hers, and he kissed her wild and hard. . . .

WHAT ARE *LOVESWEPT* ROMANCES?

They are stories of true romance and touching emotion. We believe those two very important ingredients are constants in our highly sensual and very believable stories in the *LOVESWEPT* line. Our goal is to give you, the reader, stories of consistently high quality that may sometimes make you laugh, sometimes make you cry, but are always fresh and creative and contain many delightful surprises within their pages.

Most romance fans read an enormous number of books. Those they truly love, they keep. Others may be traded with friends and soon forgotten. We hope that each *LOVESWEPT* romance will be a treasure—a "keeper." We will always try to publish

LOVE STORIES YOU'LL NEVER FORGET
BY AUTHORS YOU'LL ALWAYS REMEMBER

The Editors

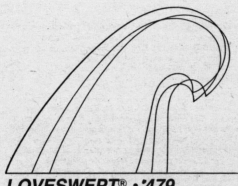

LOVESWEPT® • '479

Sandra Chastain
Silver Bracelets

 BANTAM BOOKS
NEW YORK · TORONTO · LONDON · SYDNEY · AUCKLAND

SILVER BRACELETS

A Bantam Book / June 1991

If you would be interested in receiving protective vinyl
covers for your Loveswept books, please write to this address
for information:

Loveswept
Bantam Books
P.O. Box 985
Hicksville, NY 11802

ISBN 0-553-44133-7

Published simultaneously in the United States and Canada

Bantam Books are published by Bantam Books, a division
of Bantam Doubleday Dell Publishing Group, Inc. Its trademark, consisting of the words "Bantam Books" and the
portrayal of a rooster, is Registered in U.S. Patent and
Trademark Office and in other countries. Marca Registrada.
Bantam Books, 666 Fifth Avenue, New York, New York
10103.

*For Marian Oaks
because she gave me Sarah
and a whole lot more.*

One

Sarah played the beam of her flashlight back and forth through the dark apartment until she found the half-naked man handcuffed to the brass bedpost.

"Somebody here in need of a locksmith?" she asked, and swallowed her grin. This wasn't the first practical joke she'd been called out to undo, but it was the first one where the victim was wearing only underwear and socks.

"Hell, no!" The captive swung his feet to the floor and said with deadly warning in his voice, "If I need anything, it's a firing squad. Who are you? And get that light out of my eyes."

"Sarah Wilson. Sorry, I don't have a rifle on me, and I'd turn on a lamp except there doesn't seem to be one."

"There isn't. How'd you get in here?"

Sarah decided it was just as well that there was no other light. From the tone of his voice and the set of his lips she didn't think that exposing either of them to further illumination was advisable. That was all right; she'd been warned that he'd be angry.

His clipped, evenly spaced words told her that he was barely managing to control his fury. And the beam from her flashlight was more than sufficient to reveal his totally masculine, whipcord-lean body. He didn't try to cover himself. In fact, he didn't seem to notice his near nakedness.

This rescue was proving to be a bit more intense than she'd expected. Not only was his voice intimidating, but his black hair, which was too long, and heavy five o'clock shadow made him look mean. She rarely saw a man that she didn't put a label on, but this time she was having trouble deciding whether he belonged in a late night thriller movie, or on the *Outlaws of the West* calendar in her shop.

Then she realized there were two things wrong with her line of thought. First, this was Smyrna, Georgia, not Marlboro Man country. The second and more dangerous problem was that the practical joke she'd been called in to rectify didn't seem to be amusing the victim one bit. The fact that her pulse was doing the lambada while her breaths were coming in waltz time weren't helping matters at all.

She decided to try to defuse this ticking bomb before there was an explosion and she got caught in the blast. "I'm a locksmith. If you're Asa Canyon, your friend Mike sent me over. He says that you should be a good sport about losing the bet."

"Correction. I apparently don't have any friends, and I don't bet."

"Mr. Larson knows that you're upset," she went on, as if he hadn't spoken, "and he's sorry. I'm supposed to unlock the cuffs, then tell you to read the note he left for you. And, oh yes, your boots are by the door."

Asa Canyon jerked his hand and felt the pressure of the cuffs against his wrist. Fighting the pounding waves of frustration and pain that assaulted his head, he wondered how he could have let himself be fooled. He should have known something was going on when Mike turned up so unexpectedly.

They were an unlikely pair: Mike, the wealthy playboy, and Asa, the cynical ex-Marine. Mike was the only longtime friend that Asa had, and that was only because Mike made few demands. Up until this evening, the last time they'd crossed paths had been two years ago in Denver, during a ski competition. Asa had been working security and Mike had been traveling with some of the rich and famous.

Last night, they'd gone to the Chattahoochee River Company, a bar on the square for "a real man-to-man talk" over a couple of beers. Asa vaguely remembered some long earnest speech from Mike about his being a changed man, a man with a future. That discourse was followed by a wild story about running the bulls in Spain . . . and falling in love with Jeanie.

During the second beer, Mike had been very polite when he'd asked Asa to give his approval to the marriage. It wasn't that Asa had a problem with Jeanie getting married; it was marriage to Mike that Asa objected to.

Since he'd become Jeanie's stand-in father sixteen years ago, when she'd been in boarding school, their relationship had slowly evolved into that of an older brother looking after his beloved little sister. Until three months ago when she'd called and asked him to come to Smyrna, outside Atlanta, Georgia, where she'd made her home base for the past year.

She'd been heartsick over a broken love affair, and for the first time, nothing Asa could do seemed to cheer her up. That was when she'd come up with the crazy idea that since she and Asa had always been family, they might as well make it legal and get married. Asa would have told her that she was being foolish, but she'd been hurting so badly that he hadn't been able to do it. He'd given up his security job in California and come to Smyrna, where he'd eventually signed on with the County Sheriff's department. He'd known that after Jeanie had had time to think things through, she'd change her mind, just as she had with all the other grand schemes she'd ever entertained.

What he hadn't counted on was Mike changing Jeanie's mind by making her fall in love with him. Asa remembered swearing to put Mike in jail if he even thought about making a move on Jeanie. Asa wanted Jeanie to be happy, but he'd never allow her to marry a jaded playboy without a job.

Just about the time he'd realized that Mike was serious, Asa started to feel dizzy. Mike joked that it wouldn't do for Deputy Sheriff Asa Canyon's best friend to let him get arrested for drunk driving. Mike insisted on driving Asa home. After that, everything went blank.

Now Asa understood. Mike had realized that Asa would find a way to stop the marriage, and Mike had put something in his beer. Then he'd taken Asa to Jeanie's newly rented apartment, taken his clothes, and handcuffed him to the bed with his own handcuffs. Asa had only just begun to wake up when he'd heard someone opening the door.

That someone—the woman holding the flashlight—was all mixed up with the memory of last night and the absurdity of the present situation. He hadn't heard what Sarah had just said, but from the quizzical expression on her face, he had the feeling that she'd asked a question.

"Never mind about how this happened. Maybe we ought to talk about getting you loose," Sarah went on. "You have some weird friends, Mr. Canyon, if they think that this is just a simple practical joke."

"You're right. Having your best friend slip you a Mickey is no joke, lady."

"Someone drugged you?"

Sarah was starting to become a little worried. There was something very peculiar about this call. She shined the light around, trying to figure out why the name Asa Canyon sounded familiar. Aside from the bed, there wasn't another piece of furniture in the whole room, not even curtains, sheets, or a pillow. Just one very angry man, wearing nothing but socks and underwear. The only other thing in sight was the pair of boots by the door, with the envelope sticking out of one of them.

Sarah had often been accused of being too trusting. Pop had been trusting too, and she didn't know any other way to be. But this time she might be in over her head. Still, after twenty-eight years of living her life one way, she probably couldn't change, even if she wanted to. And what she wanted now was to find out more about Asa Canyon.

Never one to follow directions, Sarah had already deviated from the instructions left on her answering machine by coming out in the middle of the night instead of waiting until morning. Now she decided that the man handcuffed to the bed ought to know what the note said *before* he was free. That way, if she was going to be the object of his anger she could either run for her life or bargain for her safety.

She picked up the envelope and started toward him.

He stopped struggling with the handcuffs.

He even seemed calm now, but there was an underlying tension about him that was intensifying with every breath he took. She would have sworn that the temperature in the apartment was rising.

Looking at her sternly, he cursed—too quietly—and said, "You're right, Ms. Wilson. This isn't a practical joke. And if Mike Larson thinks that I'm going to laugh this off he's dead wrong. You just get me loose. There's someone I have to talk to right away, before she makes a very big mistake."

Uh-oh, *she*? Sarah stopped right where she was. There was a woman involved. She'd heard about bets and payoffs, but this was truly mean! She shined her light on the note and opened it. She couldn't help but glance at the contents. This wasn't a simple bet. For a long minute she debated about what she could do to cushion the blow that was coming. But she was unable to think of a thing.

Sarah couldn't bring herself to read the note out loud. It was too personal, too painful for a man like this one. She didn't need to have him tell her that he was proud. It showed in every inch of him. And almost every inch showed.

"Maybe you'd better see this," she said, finally walking over to the bed and focusing the light on the paper so that he could see.

Asa's eyes followed the words, reading, but not accepting.

Sorry, old buddy, I tried to tell you about Jeanie and me, but you wouldn't listen. We really fell in love. She didn't want to hurt you, so I tried to explain. You weren't about to let her go so I had to take drastic measures. By the time you read this in the morning, we'll be gone. Maybe you'll learn to forgive us.

Mike

P.S. I took your clothes to slow you down—in case you managed to get away.

There was a long silence.

"Are you all right?" Sarah asked.

"Unfasten these handcuffs, Ms. Locksmith."

"Maybe you ought to think about what you're planning to do," Sarah suggested. She had to delay what was sure to be a massacre if Asa Canyon caught up with his friend.

"I have thought about it."

"I know how hurt you must be, Mr. Canyon, but he says they're in love. Surely you want this Jeanie to be happy. If you love her, you have to put your own feelings aside."

"I don't have to do anything, and I'm not in love with her."

"Oh." Sarah was stumped. Was the man heartless?

"She's my . . . my ward, not my fiancée. I care about her, but love is something I don't allow."

Don't allow? That kind of thinking was so

foreign that Sarah couldn't even voice a reply. Finally pure curiosity won out and she asked, "Haven't you ever been in love?"

"Nope."

"What about your parents?"

"Don't have any."

"Everybody has parents, Mr. Canyon."

"Not me."

He meant it. Sarah couldn't imagine growing up without a family, but this man had. "But still, you have to accept the fact that your . . . your ward has run away with your friend."

"No, I don't have to accept that. The note said 'in the morning.' There's still a chance I can stop them."

"Why would you want to do that?"

He didn't answer. Instead, he stood up and began to move the bed.

"What you are doing?" She watched in astonishment as Asa Canyon dragged the entire brass bed across the carpet to the window.

"I intend to get out of this apartment," he said, kicking out the lower pane of glass in the window. "Either with your help or by rousing the entire neighborhood. It's your choice."

"Now just a minute, Mr. Canyon. You're acting like some crazy man!"

Sarah walked around and stood between him and the window. Enough was enough. He was already inviting trouble by getting in front of the window practically nude, but breaking windows could get him arrested.

"You don't want somebody to call the police and—"

"Sarah Wilson!" He silenced her protest in midsentence. "I am the police."

"Uh-oh! The police?" Then it came to her, where she'd heard that name before. He was Deputy Sheriff Asa Canyon, the new Dirty Harry of the Cobb County Sheriff's Department, the man who, on his first week on the job, single-handedly captured the trio of robbers who'd held up the Burger Barn and escaped in the restaurant manager's car. The story and his picture had been all over the papers two weeks ago.

"Deputy Sheriff Asa Canyon," he said with a threat in his voice. "And I order you to remove the cuffs."

"Oh, goodness. Yes, sir. Let me get my keys," Sarah answered, trying to think of a way to calm his fury. "They're in the toolbox somewhere."

"You don't have a single master key?"

"Not exactly. There are several different handcuff locks. It won't take long. I just have to find the right one."

"Wonderful," Asa said under his breath. "Another nice touch, Mike. All the locksmiths in the county and you pick a woman. Cute!"

Sarah froze. "I could just walk away and leave you trussed up like a Christmas turkey."

Considering the situation, this woman was probably his quickest way out. "Sorry," he said, trying to sound contrite. "Just hurry, will you?"

Sarah picked up her toolbox and slid up close to Deputy Canyon. She couldn't avoid noticing the skimpy briefs he was wearing. Impishly she decided that she'd pegged him wrong. He ought to replace the baseball pitcher lounging seductively on the billboard near her locksmith shop. The pitcher wore a pair of burgundy briefs just like the deputy's, only not nearly so well, Sarah decided with an appreciative eye.

Yes, the gossip about the new deputy had been right. She'd encountered Dirty Harry in the flesh. This was a man who skated on the fine edge of fury and now she, too, was standing on very thin ice.

Cutting her eyes away from his body she leaned closer and began to study the lock. "This is going to be a bit tricky," she said. "I can't hold the light and my tools at the same time. Without a table to set it on, there's no way to anchor it so that it shines on your wrists."

"Open the window."

"Sorry, Deputy, you can't jump with that bed attached to your arm, glass or no glass. Besides, suicide is no answer."

"We're on the ground floor," he growled. "Put the flashlight on the windowsill and close the window on it. That ought to hold it in place."

"Deputy Canyon, are you sure you know what you're suggesting? You're wearing nothing but underwear and you'll be in the spotlight. If anybody is watching, they might possibly get the idea that we're involved in something . . . kinky."

"Kinky?" he roared, then took a deep breath. "Please, Ms. Wilson"—his voice softened just enough to let Sarah catch a glimpse of his worry—"I have to get to Jeanie and make sure that she knows what she's doing. Sixteen years ago I promised her father I'd look after her, and I never go back on my word."

"Why does she need looking after? Doesn't she have a mother?"

"No!" he barked. "I'm the only family she has. Jeanie's different. She tends to take wild chances, without considering the consequences. She always has. That's why she needs me."

He was serious. He wasn't angry with this Jeanie. In fact, Sarah was beginning to understand that his attitude was more that of a father or an older brother.

Sarah put the flashlight on the sill, then twisted his hands to get a better angle. Leaning across his body, she tried to concentrate on what she was doing rather than on his very masculine shape. He tried to turn away as if he didn't want to be touched.

"Please, keep your hands turned like this, Deputy Canyon," she said. "I'm glad your wrists are slim. It makes this less painful for you and easier for me."

"I'm glad you approve. There are those who think I'm mean and lean."

She didn't think the description referred to

his physical appearance. "And are you mean?"

"No, I'm simply careful, a quality that my ex-friend Mike apparently is learning to emulate."

Asa was aware that he was thought to be a man of purpose, one who never deviated from his course. There were some who called him a loner. He saw himself as an individualist. There were some who said he had tunnel vision. He called it commitment.

He would have stopped Jeanie from eloping. He still could. But right now he was having trouble focusing on the *how*. The lady locksmith hovering over him was proving to be very distracting, and distractions were not a part of Asa Canyon's life.

Asa's rescuer was wearing faded jeans, a T-shirt that said "Locksmith's Have the Key," and a baseball cap on her head. She smelled fresh and natural, like newly mown grass, or a watermelon right after it was cut. She was even humming as if she were completely at ease. She didn't seem to have any trouble concentrating. She certainly was paying no attention to his nearly nude state.

For that he was grateful. The rough texture of her jeans grazing against his thigh was suddenly forcing his body into paying enough attention for both of them. He took a deep breath. "Aren't you done yet?"

"The first key doesn't fit." Sarah tried another. "Are these bracelets yours?"

"Yes."

"How'd your friend get them?"

"They were attached to my belt, on my pants. There was a gun there, too. I'm glad he didn't decide to take stronger measures. He could have done some real damage to my person."

Sarah silently agreed that was a good thing. His person was perfect just as it was. Shocked at her thought, she ducked her head so that Asa couldn't see the blush that heated her cheeks.

The second key didn't fit either. She slid it around the ring and pulled up a third one. This time, by working it back and forth, she was able to release the lock. The handcuff attached to the bed slid open so suddenly that she was caught off balance. As she tried to keep from falling across the deputy, another instrument attached to her key ring, a wickedly sharp pointed pick, jabbed him in the wrist.

Asa's head snapped up. "Damn!" he exclaimed, jerking his hand forward. His sudden movement wrenched the key and broke it off in the lock, at the same time sending the key ring sailing through the broken window.

"Ouch! If I'd wanted to lose a hand I'd have gnawed my way free."

"Sorry. Now you've done it! My keys are outside somewhere in the dark. I'll have to see if I can find them to open the other cuff."

"Never mind, Sarah Wilson," he said, massaging his wrist. "I'm free of the bed. That's all I have time for."

"But what about the other bracelet?"

"I have a spare key at the station. I'll get it later. Let me get dressed and I'll pay you for your trouble."

"What do you plan to wear?"

"Damn!" He glanced over at Sarah, his gaze traveling from her T-shirt, down her long legs to her scruffy sneakers.

"No way. You'd never fit."

"Well, I'll just have to make a run for it like this."

Sarah shook her head. Even with today's loose dress codes, she guessed that *this* man would be noticed.

When she turned to free her flashlight, she saw a couple standing beside a police car on the street. They were talking to the officer and pointing at the window where Sarah was standing.

"Deputy Canyon, I don't think that it's a good idea for you to go outside just now. Not unless you want to do some tall explaining. There's a Smyrna cop out there. Somebody must have heard you break the glass."

Asa glanced out at the officer and back at Sarah. "I don't suppose you have a pair of pants in that toolbox, do you?"

"Nope, sorry. But wait a minute. I may have a solution." She picked up her toolbox, turned around, and disappeared into the darkness.

Asa imagined the worst. She was breaking into another apartment. She was stealing an overcoat and he'd be arrested as a flasher. She was calling for a pizza and they'd overpower the delivery boy. She was leaving, deserting him in his hour of need.

He began to pace back and forth. A broken window, a woman with a tool chest filled with what could be considered burglary tools, and a half-nude man. Explainable maybe, but he didn't have time for any more delays. Nosy neighbors! That's why he would never live in a place like this.

Jeanie had picked out this apartment for herself, before she'd had the wild idea that they would get married. Then, before she'd even turned on the utilities, the assignment in Spain had come along. The only furniture that got moved in was the brass bed.

Asa understood Jeanie's need to be surrounded by people, to belong. He thought it had something to do with her losing her parents so early. But he was alone, too; he didn't even know who his parents were. And he'd never fallen in and out of love like a neon sign blinking on and off.

For Asa a job that involved constant travel was a calculated choice. If he didn't stay in one place very long, he couldn't get close to anyone. If he didn't allow himself to get close, he wouldn't be hurt. But for Jeanie, and Mike too, the world was their playground. They ran toward tomorrow and what it might bring.

Asa looked at his watch, the green numbers blinking at him in the darkness. Where was Sarah Wilson? *She* seemed dependable, firmly rooted in old-fashioned optimism and responsibility. Surely she hadn't abandoned him.

About the time he decided to take a chance on flashing the neighborhood she came back, holding out red coveralls with the name "Jim" embroidered on the pocket.

"Try these. They were Pop's, but I think they'll fit."

They did. Asa pulled them on and jammed his feet into his boots. He moved over to the window and glanced outside. The police officer was heading toward them. Asa didn't have time for an interrogation. There was only one quick way out. Kinky was acceptable; burglary wasn't.

"Don't scream, Sarah. Just consider this as being in the line of duty." He reached out and pulled her into his arms, capturing her lips with sureness.

For a moment she struggled.

"Cooperate, woman, please!"

Whether it was the desperate plea in his voice or her own breathless reaction to his lips, she relaxed and gave in to the kiss being delivered by a master of the art.

Her heart felt the jolt first. Then her pulse kicked in and her breathing raced. Jeanie was definitely an idiot for running away with a practical joker when she could have had this man. Sarah didn't know what to say about herself. Maybe she was a idiot, too, for there was no question that she was kissing Asa back.

By the time Asa pulled away, Sarah was glad that he was still holding her; otherwise she would have melted into a puddle at his feet.

He gave a jaunty wave to the officer, then snapped off Sarah's flashlight.

For a moment he gazed at Sarah in silence. He could hear the sound of her breathing.

"Thanks for not screaming. Let's get out of here before the people watching decide to join our party. How much do I owe you?"

"Oh, the kiss is free. Since it was in the line of duty."

"I meant for the locksmith's call."

Still half stunned by the kiss, Sarah freed her flashlight and followed the deputy as he moved out the door and across the lawn to the parking area.

"A call after midnight is forty dollars," she said. "But unless you're into bartering, I don't know how you expect to pay me. I'll send you a bill."

He swore again. "I'll pay you tomorrow. But forty dollars isn't enough. You came out after midnight, to a strange apartment, to free a man in handcuffs and you're only going to charge forty dollars?"

"That's the price my dad set and that's what you owe me."

"Then why didn't your dad make the call? I might have been a criminal. You know you could have been in big trouble." He frowned as he allowed himself to notice how attractive she was.

He'd vaguely realized she was tall enough that he hadn't had to lean down to kiss her and that her breasts had felt generous pressing against his chest. He'd seen honesty reflected in her eyes and felt the warmth of skin that, in the shadows, was the color of honey. She'd been more of an imagined impression based on touch and smell, until that impression crystallized into a woman whose lips softened and responded to his kiss.

Now in the lighted parking area he could see that her short hair, peeking out from beneath her cap, was light brown rather than blond. She wasn't wearing any makeup and her face had the warm, healthy color of a woman who spent time outdoors. She was looking at him with an expression that he couldn't identify.

"My father couldn't come," she said quietly. "My father is dead. And you aren't a criminal. You're just worried about someone you care for."

He felt a twinge of guilt for his choice of words and started to say he was sorry, but she cut him off.

"Jeanie must be a terribly insensitive person," Sarah couldn't help commenting. "I don't understand why she didn't tell you herself if she wanted to marry your friend."

"Because I wouldn't have approved of the marriage, and they both knew it. It's too soon for Jeanie to make that kind of decision. When she left for Spain she was still hurting from an affair gone bad. . . . Damn! Where's my Silver Girl? Ah, no, not her, too."

Sarah thought he was going to yell. Somehow she knew that Asa Canyon was a man who didn't cry. "Please don't be so distressed,"

Sarah consoled him. "You may not understand it now, but you'll have to look on your girl running away as happening for the best."

"My girl?" He laughed. "She couldn't leave on her own. She had to have help." He slapped his thigh, then groaned. "My pants and my keys—they're both gone."

"The note said that she and your friend Mike are in love. You can't fight an emotion strong enough to force him into this kind of action."

"Mike wouldn't be caught dead in my truck. He drives a BMW. But you're right. He took her all right, so I couldn't follow. You'd think he'd have at least told me where he left her, since he's so good at letter writing. It's bad enough that he's taken Jeanie, but my Silver Girl? That's a low blow."

Sarah realized that Silver Girl was not the woman, but his truck. She giggled, half in relief and half in disbelief.

"You have a very strange sense of humor," Asa growled. "Do you have a car to match?"

Her sense of humor might be strange, he concluded, as he stared at her, but her lips, still curved in a smile, were nice. Wide, full and honest, they matched her open face. Everything about Sarah Wilson said that what you see is what you get. And honesty was a characteristic that was in short supply in his life at the moment.

If he weren't so concerned about Jeanie, he just might—no. Women were rarely what they seemed and he'd sworn long ago not to try to figure them out. He glanced at Sarah. She didn't seem worried. In fact, he had a sneaking suspicion that she was the kind of "girl next door" who could be a coconspirator, the kind who didn't scream when you put a frog in her lunch box. But that girl-next-door look didn't fit the kiss they'd just shared, or the open way she'd participated.

"Do I have a car? Not a car," Sarah was saying. "A van, and you might say it matches my sense of humor. Why?"

"I'm commandeering it. Let's go!"

"Oh, good. A police chase. I thought that only happened in the movies! If you have in mind tearing through the city streets, I feel it only fair to warn you that the fastest he'll go is 54 miles per hour. Anything more and he rebels."

"He? You have a car you refer to as he?"

"I do. His name is Henry. Helpful Henry. You call your truck Girl, why can't I call my van Henry?"

"Where is it?" Then he saw it. The van had once been a bright fire-truck red. Now it was battered and bruised, the color faded. The sign on its side, a yellow smiley face and letters that proclaimed *HELP IS ON THE WAY*, was new and shiny. He groaned. "Never mind. Get in. I'll drive."

"I think you'd better let me," Sarah protested.

"I know where I'm going and I'll get us there faster." He figured Mike and Jeanie had returned to Smyrna together, and were staying in Jeanie's old apartment. He'd get over there and play it by ear.

"Suit yourself, but don't say I didn't warn you."

Sarah unlocked the van, slung her tool chest in the back and climbed in the passenger side, handing the keys to the deputy.

He managed to start the engine, but there wasn't enough room for Asa's long legs. To add to the problem, the play in the pedals was so bad that he couldn't keep an even amount of pressure applied to either one. The result was a van that jumped and sputtered past the police car still sitting in the street. By the time Asa finally figured out the secret to keeping Harry running, the police car had fallen in behind the van and was following what had to be, even to Asa, a suspicious vehicle.

Another minute passed and the blue lights began to flash. The police car moved up beside the van and the officer motioned for them to pull over.

"Ah, hell!" Asa said, but complied. "I don't even have my identification. It's in my wallet, in my pants, wherever they are."

The officer got out of the car and walked slowly toward the window. "Will you get out of the vehicle, sir?"

Sarah had already ducked her head to smother a giggle. She watched as Asa caught the dangling cuff in his hand and palmed it as best he could, opened the door, and slid out. She could have identified herself and brought the suspicion to an end, but since Asa Canyon wanted to be in charge, she'd let him.

"There's been a misunderstanding," Asa began, remembering how many times he'd heard just such a lame excuse. If he ever got his hands on his ex-friend again he'd rip him limb from limb. "I know this will be hard for you to believe, Officer . . . ?"

"Officer Martin, sir."

"Officer Martin, my wallet has been stolen, along with my—" he started to say "clothes" and changed it to "truck."

"Are you telling me that you don't have a license?"

"Of course I have a license. I just don't have it with me. It's in my wallet. Ah, for crying out loud!"

"Sorry, sir. Please turn around, put your hands against the side, and spread your legs."

"Now listen here!" Asa folded his arms across his chest and rocked back and forth on the balls of his feet, feeling like a defensive linebacker psyching himself into a mood to kill. "My name is Asa Canyon and I'm a deputy sheriff."

"Yes, sir. Are you saying that this is your vehicle?"

"No, it belongs to Sarah Wilson."

"Oh? And you borrowed it?"

"No. Yes. Ask her," he roared.

Officer Martin stepped aside and peered into the van. "Are you in there, Sarah?"

"Yep." Sarah straightened and took a deep breath, hoping she was doing the right thing. "And this man is trying to kidnap Henry. I'd like him arrested, please."

Two

Asa Canyon growled and made a move toward Sarah.

Officer Martin responded by drawing his gun and stepping between Asa and the van. "I wouldn't do that, sir."

Sarah took one look at the set of Asa's lips and decided that her plan to give the deputy some cooling off time while Jeanie and Mike got away was not a viable idea.

Mike's life might have been in danger before. Now he was definitely a dead man. And she was about to join him.

"Tell this officer the truth, Sarah. Please?"

Sarah never had much patience with a man who thought he had all the answers, and the deputy did need to learn he wasn't always right. If Mike •and Jeanie were in love, they ought to be allowed to get married without the long arm of the law interfering.

On the other hand, what did she really know? Asa had said that Jeanie wasn't over an affair. And the note had said that she didn't want to hurt him. Maybe all of this anger was more than just worry. Maybe the affair had been between Jeanie and the deputy. Sarah slid out of the van and touched Paul Martin on the arm.

"It's all right, Paul," she said. Turning to Asa, she added belligerently, "But next time before you start hijacking somebody's vehicle you might just *ask* for their help. People around here are usually willing to give a hand to a person in need."

She faced the officer again. "Paul, meet Deputy Asa Canyon, with the Cobb Sheriff's department. We're on an emergency call."

"Are you sure, Sarah?" Paul was not entirely convinced.

"I'm sure. I was just—never mind. He really is Deputy Canyon."

Paul Martin took another look at Asa and grimaced. "I'm very sorry, sir. I've only seen your picture in the paper. I didn't recognize you. We've been having a lot of burglaries around here and there was something really weird going on in an apartment back there. I thought—"

"Never mind what you thought," Asa began.

Sarah wasn't certain who would be the ranking officer, a patrolman or a deputy sheriff, but she felt bad about placing her friend Paul in an awkward situation. "Thank you

Paul, for checking on me. We really do need to go now."

Sure, Sarah. See you later at the softball game." He turned back to Asa and held the van door open. "Sorry again, sir. I didn't know who you were."

"That's okay, Officer. You can never be too careful."

Sarah decided that she'd better not comment on what had just happened. Paul may have accepted her story, but sooner or later he was going to wonder about a deputy sheriff with no identification, who was wearing her father's coveralls, cowboy boots, and, one handcuff.

Asa climbed inside and coaxed Henry back to life. He took Atlanta Road past the downtown Smyrna revitalization project that would result in a new business section laid out like an old-fashioned village. By the time he got through the Platinum Triangle intersection, which lay between Smyrna and the city of Atlanta, he had figured out the van's peculiarities.

"I take it you know Officer Martin?"

"Yep. I'm acquainted with most everybody in Smyrna. When you've lived here all your life, you get to know folks pretty well. We tend to look after one another."

"Well I hope that you don't have any other friends interested in your well-being because I really don't have time to stop." Asa pulled onto the expressway that circled the outer perimeter of Atlanta and headed east.

"No, Paul will pass the word. But I think you should know that Harry's fuel gauge doesn't work and we probably ought to get gas if you're planning to go very far."

"Now you tell me." Asa glanced at the service station he was passing on the right. He knew the next exit didn't have one but that the one after that did. He let out a sigh of relief. Still his sigh came too soon. The van sputtered twice and coasted to a stop at the side of the road.

"Sorry, Deputy, but don't you get the feeling that maybe somebody is trying to tell you that you ought not to be making this trip? Why don't you let them go? You're only going to make things worse."

"Sarah, Mike knows that I don't allow anybody to interfere with me doing my duty."

"Spoken like a true officer of the law, Sergeant Friday. Or is it Sergeant Preston of the Yukon? Maybe you should send for your faithful horse and dog to get through the snowdrifts up ahead." This time she didn't need a flashlight to see his brows draw together in a thundering expression. "Take it easy."

"Take it easy?"

"Somebody will come along who knows us."

Not if Asa could help it. Before he stayed long enough for somebody to know him, he moved on. He'd learned about moving on by the time he was ten years old and had already been returned to the orphanage by three sets of foster parents that he could remember. He didn't know how many homes he'd been through as a baby.

His own mother had taught him the first lesson by leaving him on the steps of a church. The others, well, they had tried, but Asa hadn't let them get close. And one after another, they'd returned him to the orphanage, as if he were a pair of shoes that didn't fit.

Eventually, when he was ten years old, he figured it out. Everybody in his life was temporary. After that he made so much trouble that he was sent to a group home where he lived until he graduated from high school. The next day he'd joined the Marines, and he'd been on the move ever since. He'd learned the hard way that love didn't last and people were temporary.

Then Jeanie became his responsibility. Yet, even then he'd always managed to keep their association in perspective. She was in his charge for a while. He'd understood that one day she'd leave, too—but not this way.

Sarah felt Asa's frustration and pursed her lips. So he didn't want help. That didn't surprise her. "Well," she finally offered, "if you feel like walking, there's a gas can in the back."

Asa took the can, strode briskly down the road, then stopped and turned back, a sheepish expression on his face. "Do you have any money?"

Sarah didn't answer. One more word and Deputy Canyon would explode. Silently she fished a crumpled ten dollar bill from her pocket and handed it to him. He stalked off, measuring the distance in such long strides that anybody would have been forced to run to keep up.

A car pulled into the emergency lane and stopped in front of Asa. The driver, an elderly man wearing overalls and smoking a cigar, stuck his head out and asked, "That's Sarah's van out of gas back there, isn't it? Get in, son."

Any other time Asa would have kept on walking, but tonight he had no seconds to lose. He crawled in the car and thanked the old man.

"Don't worry about it, son. Not a man or woman in Smyrna who wouldn't stop to give Sarah Wilson a hand. Fine girl she is. Not a better shortstop in the state when she was in high school. Lost out on an out-of-state college scholarship looking after her dad. Folks 'round here think a lot of Sarah."

The old man talked faster than he drove, and he wouldn't win a race at either one, Asa thought wryly. Several minutes lapsed before Asa filled the gas can and managed to get back to Sarah's van. He emptied the gas into the tank, then thanked the man who had already told him more about Sarah than he ever wanted to know, and drove off.

Asa tried to concentrate on Jeanie and how he was going to convince her that marrying Mike was a bad idea. He'd offer to help her furnish the apartment she'd rented, and if she wanted to open a nice little photography studio, he'd help her do that, too.

He pulled into a gas station and began filling up, all the while planning his argument. But a little voice inside his mind told him that Jeanie wouldn't be happy in a studio. She wasn't like Sarah, who had taken over her father's business and made a life for herself in the place where she'd grown up. Sarah knew everybody in town and everybody looked after her. Sarah Wilson wouldn't need somebody like him around.

And she had a mind of her own. She'd stood right up to him. He thought of her threat to have him arrested and smiled.

He'd stolen her van and probably compromised her before her friend. He hadn't even thanked her for helping him. But the thing that kept sticking in his mind the most was the kiss, the way she'd returned it and how her lips had felt beneath his own. He tried to put it out of his mind. But not thinking made the remembering more vivid.

This was the kind of situation he usually backed away from. Sarah was trouble. But this time he couldn't leave. He couldn't move on to another assignment in another city. He had to stay here until he was sure Jeanie was all right. He'd promised her father that.

But the long-legged shortstop who gave up her scholarship to take care of her dad interfered with his concentration on the problem at hand.

After Asa paid the attendant he climbed back inside and coaxed Henry to life. "Sarah," he began, "I'm sorry if I've caused a problem for you tonight. I know this all seems . . . strange."

"Strange? Nah. Practically every night I get a call to rescue a bridegroom handcuffed to a bedpost. But you may be the first one wearing maroon drawers."

Asa groaned.

"Actually, Deputy Canyon, I don't mind a bit of friendly practical joking, but kidnapping? If that's what you have in for mind for Jeanie, I have to say I draw the line there."

"I am not planning to kidnap Jeanie. I'm simply planning to prevent her from making a rash decision."

"This Jeanie, how old is she?"

"Jeanie's twenty-nine."

"A year older than me. I thought she must be about sixteen from the way you were talking. How come she needs rescuing constantly?"

"Because she's a poor judge of men and every time she's disappointed, she runs off to some foreign country."

"Well now, I'd say she wants to get away from you pretty bad to go to those extremes."

"Not from me. And she isn't always trying to get away. Sometimes she's trying to get to something. She's a photographer."

"How'd she get to be your responsibility?"

"Her father was my commanding officer in 'Nam. He was a widower. Sixteen years ago he died saving my life and I gave him my word that I'd look after his daughter."

"And you still are. Maybe she doesn't need looking after any more."

"Yes she does! Sooner or later I thought she'd get ready to settle down and live a normal life. But she has this thing about making pictures in parts of the world where no woman should go. Now she's found a willing partner."

"Is she any good at what she does?"

"She's a fine photographer. It's picking men that she isn't very good at."

"I can believe that." Sarah decided anybody who could reject Deputy Canyon had to be a poor judge of men.

With pride, he told her how Jeanie had made the cover of a weekly magazine with photographs of a war-torn nation.

Sarah didn't mean to gasp, but the thought of a woman slipping into a battle zone was terrifying. Still, Jeanie obviously went after what she wanted, whether it was a man or a picture, and Sarah could understand that. She could even understand Jeanie eloping, if that was the only way.

Sarah had never been in love but, like Jeanie, she was given to following her heart rather than her head, and she could tell that they were both dealing with a man who would always take the sensible approach to every action.

"If she wants your friend Mike, why are you trying to stop them?"

"You'd have to know Mike. His family has more money than he'll ever spend. He doesn't have to do anything he doesn't want to and that's what he's done for the last thirty-four years—nothing. It seems that he and Jeanie ran into each other in Spain while he was running the bulls. He didn't run very fast. According to him, Jeanie rescued him from certain death."

"And they fell in love."

"Infatuation more likely. But marriage? No! Mike is a man with no ambition. It's not that I don't like Mike, I do. He'd give you the shirt off his back. His problem is that he's never set a goal and reached it in his life."

"Except this time," Sarah said. No-ambition Mike must have more get up and go than Asa thought. Mike wanted Jeanie and he knew Asa well enough to know that he'd never allow their marriage. So Mike had come with a plan. Talk first, but if all else failed, get Jeanie in a dramatic, off-the-wall way that Asa couldn't have anticipated.

Sarah smiled. She liked a man who could slip a Mickey to a deputy sheriff. Reluctantly she admitted that she even liked a woman who could fall in love with a guy who ran the bulls.

About Asa Canyon, she was confused.

Sarah glanced over at the man with the silver handcuffs still attached to one wrist. There was real dedication in this deputy sheriff, a finely tuned sense of honor and justice that was rare. She'd been right about him when she thought he belonged in the Old

West. Except he wouldn't be the outlaw. He'd be the sheriff.

Still, there was something about that historical picture that didn't quite fit. He was a man who protected his woman, all right, but in his burgundy shorts and with a kiss that came on like gangbusters, he was definitely a man of the nineties.

As the van lurched down Riverside Drive, Sarah realized the Old West sheriff image wasn't the only thing that wasn't completely correct. Her red van, with its smiley face on the side, stuck out like a sore thumb in the rich neighborhood. The houses they were passing were so far from the road that they couldn't be seen and the only thing on the mailboxes were numbers.

"Your fiancée must do pretty well with her pictures, Deputy Canyon."

"You mean the ritzy area? She's been living with a friend, an airline stewardess. They share a carriage house, as much sharing as they do when both of them are gone all the time."

As he pulled into a driveway, Sarah swallowed a protest.

Help is on the way, she thought, and wondered who needed help the most. Looking at the back of the Tudor mansion with burglar bars and carriage house, Sarah decided it might be the deputy. He was convinced that he should come between Jeanie and the man she loved in order to repay a debt of honor.

Acting totally on impulse, Sarah leaned over,

slid the dangling bracelet across the steering wheel and snapped it closed.

"What the hell do you think you're doing?"

"Saving you."

"Saving me from what?"

"Ruining three lives."

"The only life I'm going to ruin is Mike's. I care too much for Jeanie to ever hurt her. Now get this cuff off the steering wheel so I can stop her."

Sarah gasped. She'd been right about the affair. Deputy Canyon was in love with Jeanie. All his protesting was because he wasn't over the affair. Acting before she thought was something Sarah often did, sometimes with disastrous consequences. But she always corrected her mistakes.

Quickly she turned to her toolbox and began to fish around for the spare set of keys she usually carried. But she couldn't find it. Her heart was beating too fast and she was unable see very well. Finally she switched on the flashlight.

"Quit stalling, Sarah."

Asa was beginning to sound very angry. And it looked as if he had every reason. "Deputy, I don't know how to tell you this, but there isn't another key in this toolbox. You'll have to come back to my place with me and I'll get the spare."

"Then you'd better get inside that carriage house and make sure that Jeanie doesn't move until I get loose."

"Are you sure? Yes, of course. I'll stop her."

When the private neighborhood security squad arrived to apprehend the intruders, Asa had to explain why he was handcuffed to the steering wheel of a locksmith's van, while the locksmith was attempting to break into someone's house.

It wasn't Jeanie who was eventually roused by the commotion, but her roommate. She explained that Jeanie and Mike had taken a late night flight to Africa where Jeanie had a new assignment. After the security men were finally satisfied that Asa's concern was for the safety of his ward, they agreed to let them go.

It was nearly morning when Asa, following Sarah's directions, drove the van past a sprawling white house and around a stand of pines to a bright red barn.

"Where do you live, Sarah? I'd like to get home as soon as possible. I'm tired and hungry and ready for bed."

"Yes. Well, you do have a bed, but from what I could see back there, you have no other furniture, no curtains, no food and no—"

"More patience!" he roared. "That isn't where I live, Sarah. Jeanie rented that apartment and bought that bed. I live in a log cabin on a lake. Now get these cuffs off me, or I'll sit on this horn until every cow in that barn goes berserk."

"Yes, sir. Just a minute." Sarah climbed out, opened the gate and disappeared through a door in the side of the barn. In a minute she was back with a pair of very large clippers. With two snips, the handcuffs were clear of the steering wheel and both Asa's hands were free.

Sarah looked over at Asa. His five o'clock shadow had gotten darker, making him look even more stern. He was tired and she couldn't really resent him for being short-tempered. She was sure that he was blaming her for his not having stopped the elopement.

"I'm sorry," she began. "One way or another, I always seem to make a mess out of dealing with men, unless they're on a ball field. Don't suppose you'd like to play a quick game of basketball, would you?"

He looked around at the trim red barn and the white fence anchored by two huge steel posts in front of the door. "At six-thirty in the morning?"

"No, I suppose that wouldn't be a good idea. But I could make coffee. I'm not a good cook, but the coffee will be hot, and I do owe you something."

For a moment Asa laid his head across his arms on the steering wheel. He must be more tired than he realized. He didn't want to leave. There was something appealing about Sarah Wilson, something that touched him in a way that he couldn't even put a name to.

He didn't know how this had happened, but he'd let down his guard and she'd silently slipped into his mind without his permission. He didn't have time or room in his life for a woman, certainly not an innocent like Sarah. It had to be because he was tired and hungry.

"Coffee, Deputy? Maybe some food?"

There was a soft coolness in the air. Beyond the van was the stand of pine trees between her mother's house and the barn, and the apple trees she and her father had planted when she was six. Pop had built the barn the next year, facing the trees. The cows would like the view, he'd said.

Sarah felt the lump in her throat that always came when she thought of her father and the good times they'd shared. This place had become her private haven during the time he was so sick, and afterwards when she'd needed a place where she could heal. Now she was asking a man inside and that felt right, too.

She stood waiting, expecting Henry's engine to come to life any minute. But it didn't. There was only silence. She opened the barn door and started inside. She didn't really expect Asa to accept her invitation. But then she heard him climbing out and following.

"Just one question, Dame Galahad. I may be tired, but I'm an old country boy and if I'm not mistaken, this is called a barn. What exactly do you eat for breakfast—hay?"

"Sorry, no hay. There isn't a cow on the place." She snapped on the lights.

Asa blinked. He closed his eyes and opened them again. From the time he'd first cracked his eyelids in the wee hours of this morning he'd felt as if he'd fallen down Alice's rabbit hole. Now he was certain.

What he saw wasn't a barn with a dirt floor and stalls. There were no cows or animals of any kind. Instead, he was standing at the edge of a basketball court, complete with a shiny polished floor and two baskets mounted on backboards.

"I don't believe it," he said, wide-eyed. "I must be dreaming. I'll wake up in a minute and find that this has all been a dream."

"Last night wasn't a dream," Sarah said softly. "Neither is this."

Sarah's voice echoing about the large room brought him dramatically back to earth. She was still standing just inside the barn door, waiting for him to get over his surprise.

"When I was in high school my dad and I turned the barn into what my mother called our playhouse. Pop couldn't play, but he liked having my friends around. Two years after he died I turned the hayloft into an apartment and moved out here."

"You live in a gym?"

"Not exactly." She gave a warm laugh. "Though I know it must look that way. Come with me. I'll show you." She led him across the court to a set of stairs leading up to the second floor.

Asa decided that watching Sarah climb the steps unsettled him about as much as the barn below. Normally Asa was very good at masking his thoughts and his facial expression, but this morning he felt as if he'd borrowed someone else's body and nothing fit.

First he'd had too much to drink with Mike. He'd lost Jeanie. He'd lost his clothes. He'd lost his Silver Girl. Now, for a reason even he couldn't figure out, he was about to have breakfast in a hayloft.

At the top of the steps Sarah opened a door, flipping off the lights below.

"If you'd like to take a shower and clean up while I cook breakfast, the bathroom is through there." Sarah flicked her head toward a corridor leading off the combination kitchen, dining and living room in which she was standing.

"Shower?" Asa finally roused himself enough to respond.

He was having a hard time following her conversation. Take a shower in *her* shower? Not this guy. There was something too personal about the idea. Then he shook his head at his hesitation. Hell, she was only offering the use of her shower—not her bed, or her body. He didn't know why he was having such a problem with the suggestion.

"Sure," Sarah replied. "This has been a long night. Personally I always feel better when I'm fresh and clean, don't you?"

Sarah could see that Asa looked a bit stunned. Losing the woman he had sworn to look after had left him confused. For a person like Asa, that must be a real blow to his pride.

Sarah was certain that he never lost a crook, or misplaced his squad car, or forgot his gun. He was too careful. This breach of procedure was bound to weigh heavily on his mind. He was hurting.

Hurt was something she considered herself an expert in. She'd had enough experience concealing it and dealing with others who did the same. Sarah moved into the kitchen and began removing things from the refrigerator. She kept talking.

"There's an extra toothbrush in the medicine cabinet and a razor. There's a robe hanging on the back of the door. It will be too short, of course, but . . ." She took a quick look at the sheriff, realized that she was overwhelming him, and slowed down.

"Sorry, Deputy Canyon. I don't normally talk like this. I guess you may have guessed I'm nervous. I mean you're the first man I've invited up here. I'm not quite sure what to say to you that won't sound dumb."

She *was* nervous, Asa agreed. Well, she wasn't the only one. It didn't take a Supreme Court justice to know that they were both out of their element. She was right about one thing. He felt like hell. His head was still vibrating, and his stomach was grumbling. Come to think of it, he couldn't remember having eaten since yesterday morning.

"I'm sorry. Nothing you could say would sound dumb. After what happened last night, I'd believe you had E.T. hidden in the closet and Starman in your shower."

"Oh no," she quipped. "Downstairs, maybe, but not up here. This is my home. This is personal. Besides, I've never met an alien. Have you?"

"No. I've met a few characters that I was suspicious of, but no confirmed cases. Are you making coffee?"

"Yes," she replied, astonished that the man

actually had a sense of humor. "According to Pop, a cup of my coffee will really give you a reason to be out of sorts."

"I can't believe it's that bad."

"It is, trust me."

"I'll find a way to live with it. I always do."

"Sugar?" she questioned, biding her time for when she could ask him to elaborate on his answer, which she guessed had nothing to do with her coffee.

"Yes, and cream, too."

That was another surprise. Sarah would have bet this man took his coffee with gunpowder and nails. She placed the sugar and milk on a small round table beside a window. She broke two eggs into a bowl and whipped them with her fork. "How?"

"How what?"

She dropped bread into the toaster, and poured the eggs into a skillet. "How do you find a way to live with things?"

"It's mental. I'm not sure that I can explain. I go over a situation again and again, until I understand. Then, once I have it straight in my mind, I deal with it."

"Not me," Sarah said, shaking her head. "I make my decision instantly, then worry it to death. I took an art class once. We were drawing with charcoal. The teacher thought my simple sketch of an old woman was nice. Then I kept going over it, adding, smearing, until it was awful. . . . If you're not going to clean up you might as well sit down. You're making me nervous again, standing over me."

Asa hadn't realized that he'd gradually moved nearer and nearer as Sarah talked. "I guess I'm trying to understand. What's the connection, Sarah, between your art class and my anger?"

"By the time I finished, my drawing had turned into a real muddle. The instructor said I worried it to death. After that I decided that I'm better suited to physical expression than artistic."

"Yes," he agreed, taking in the smooth long lines of her body and remembering the gym downstairs. "That works for you, but I've never had much time for physical outlets for my emotions."

"Not even with Jeanie?"

This time he didn't even make an attempt to hold back his laughter. "Sarah Wilson, believe it or not, without a camera in her hand, Jeanie was as physical as a dress mannequin in a department store window."

"But your affair? Didn't you ever? I mean, surely—" Sarah cut off her own question. She didn't want to know about their relationship.

"Sarah, the affair I was referring to wasn't between Jeanie and me. She'd been with some journalist for over a year when they broke up. I never even kissed her. Well, that's not exactly right. She kissed me once, when she suffered her first broken heart. Shocked the hell out of us both. She was twenty and had too much wine. I wasn't the man she wanted to be kissing and neither of us ever mentioned it again. Shows you what an impression my kisses make."

Sarah slid the skillet from the burner and looked at Asa. "Oh, how awful. I'm so sorry."

"Well, let's face it, Sarah. I'd make a terrible husband." Asa was confused by the depth of Sarah's concern. He didn't normally open up to a woman, but she seemed so determined to share his great disappointment that he found himself responding in a way he never had before.

"Oh, but you're wrong. I mean you kiss wonderfully well. Of course I don't have much to compare it to, but I thought it was . . . sweet."

"Sweet?" He gripped the countertop with his fingers. "Sarah, no man wants his kisses to be sweet. If you're going to try to make me feel better about what happened tonight, at least use a passionate term to describe my kiss."

"Like what? I'm afraid that I'm not very well versed in love talk."

"Like exciting, or hot."

Sarah knew that in spite of what he was saying, the stern man staring at her was only using her to take the brunt of his anger. She was the one who ought to be angry. She wanted him to see her, instead of someone she was substituting for. Someone who, in Sarah's personal opinion, was an idiot when it came to Asa Canyon. Any woman who'd willingly give up his kisses must be an idiot. She herself was having trouble remaining calm just because he was standing near her. Thinking of how he'd kissed her made her situation even worse. Her emotions scrambled in forty different directions.

The kiss in front of the window had been a necessary diversion, nothing more. She'd intended to ignore it, seal its devastating effect away where it would remain until she could bring it out again later and examine it. But her plan hadn't worked any better than Asa's. Her brain, like her charcoal drawing, was becoming more and more muddled as she tried not to think about the kiss.

Sarah reached over to remove the toast from the toaster. That was a mistake. It only brought her closer to the man she was trying not to think about.

She froze.

Asa turned off the burner on the stove. He caught Sarah's arms, one in each hand, and turned neatly around so that he was leaning against the counter and she was leaning against him.

Their gazes met and locked, her lashes fluttering for a long minute. Then, slowly, but with certainty, she understood. The first kiss was official business. This was personal. He was asking for solace, for comfort, and she could give it. He'd been hurt and hurt was something she could soothe, if not forever, at least for now.

With an almost imperceptible nod of agreement, she slid her hands up his chest and around his neck. "I'm sure there *is* a better word to describe your kiss. If you'll give me another demonstration, I'll try to come up with something . . . hot."

This time Asa didn't blink. His body warmed from being pressed against Sarah's curves. The unexpected tingling sensation that came as a result seemed to vibrate down his chest to his thighs.

"You're an unusual person, Sarah Wilson—nice, caring, kind."

"Yes, I think I am. And so are you."

"Most people don't think of me as any of those things. Steadfast, determined, and unbending, maybe. But nice? I'm not sure I could ever be that."

"I'm sure." She looked up at him, her sincerity shining in her eyes. "Otherwise we wouldn't be here."

"Yes, we would. You see me as some wounded sparrow you've brought home to nurse back to life. I'm not."

"Will you please stop talking and kiss me again? I know it's terribly forward of me, but I think it might make both of us feel better. Of course if you'd rather not, I'd understand."

"I've been honest with you, Sarah. I'm not known as a gentle man. Are you sure that you want to get involved with me?" Asa asked in a voice so unsteady that even he didn't recognize it.

"I'm sure. Kiss me, Asa Canyon."

Asa wanted to turn around and leave. He wanted to push himself away from her and run down the steps and out into the pasture beyond. But her eyes held him. And her concern warmed and touched that secret part of him that had been frozen for such a long time.

He groaned and felt the ice begin to melt.

Three

This time when he kissed her it wasn't for the benefit of someone watching. It wasn't in the line of duty. It certainly wasn't planned. With a will of its own, his mouth brushed her lips, slipped over them, meeting, capturing, recognizing the rightness of their touch and melding with them at last in a pool of hot sensation. He didn't rush, nor did his hands cradle and caress. They were simply together, as if their being together had been meant all along.

When Asa finally drew back, Sarah looked up at him, her eyes dreamy. "See? I told you so. You kiss wonderfully."

He tried not to smile, though it was very hard to resist the urge. He felt confused and to cover his uncertainty he railed out at Sarah. "For God's sake, Sarah, do you always go around picking up strange men and kissing them?"

"No. Do you always pretend you don't like something when you do?"

"Of course I don't. We're not talking about pleasure here."

"You may not be, but I am."

"What you're doing is issuing me an invitation."

She slipped her hand around his neck. "Exactly. And there's an RSVP included."

"Sorry, babe. I never learned much about etiquette. The only response I have to give you is a warning."

"You already responded, Asa. You kissed me back. Kissing a person is a kind of promise." She didn't pull away. She was aware of his reaction to her body. His maleness lay hard against her and she was feeling pleasant little twinges where they touched. One sensation was a part of another, which led to another, and another.

"What kind of promise?" His arms, with a will of their own, slid around her and rested rebelliously on her lower back.

"Well, I think that when a kiss is right, it's like making music. I feel it in my body, in your body, as if our very skin is carrying the melody. Like the wind in the trees, like sunlight dappling the water, like the smell of Christmas."

Asa knew he ought to pull back and leave. He knew that he'd already gone one step too far. But he couldn't seem to make himself go. Instead of growling at her, he said, his voice was low and tight, "Sunlight? Christmas? All that from a kiss?"

"I don't think you've had much time to hear the songs in the trees, or smell Christmas, have you, Deputy Canyon?"

"No, I guess I don't know much about those things." He lowered his head, brushing her lips again. As she parted her mouth to welcome him, he decided that this morning the taste of coffee was like ambrosia.

Sarah lifted her head and returned his smile. "Ready?"

He blinked. "Ready?"

"For breakfast?" she answered, freeing herself from his arms and looking at him with pleasure.

"My stomach seems to be growling," he agreed, "but I think my body may have other preferences at the moment."

Sarah followed his line of vision to the obvious erection he made no attempt to conceal. She liked that. He responded to her body and that was natural. Why should two people be embarrassed over expressing desire? Her own body wasn't shy in revealing its aroused state.

"Anticipation can be half the pleasure. Take Christmas. Wondering what's inside the box is almost always as exciting as actually having the gift, don't you think?"

Was it? Asa didn't know. If he wanted a woman, he usually got her. If she wasn't interested, that was fine, too. But he'd never,

ever, discussed the wanting so honestly before.

"Do you feel better?" Sarah asked. She felt Asa's tension slide away. His body seemed to loosen and relax. He was letting go, allowing the frustration to disappear.

"Better?"

"I mean I can understand why what happened threatened your confidence. I just thought that you ought to know that you have nothing to worry about. You're a caring person. Any woman would be lucky to have you look after her."

Her words hit him like a snowball, splattering against his face and showering against his chest. "You mean all this was just to make me feel better?"

"Well . . ." She considered her answer and decided that she wasn't fooling anybody, including herself. "That's how it started. At least that's what I told myself. Truthfully, I kind of forgot that it was for you. I mean I was sharing the feeling so much that I lost sight of your needs and just enjoyed it."

He forced himself to remember that though she was twenty-eight, she obviously didn't know what she was doing. "Sarah, do you always make people feel better?"

"If you mean do I go around kissing men like this, no. This is my first time. Oh, I've had dates, boyfriends, but nobody has filled my stomach with butterflies since I was seventeen. But I guess that's not what you're talking about, is it?"

Butterflies? Hell, if she had a stomach full of butterflies he was battling with a pit of giant condors.

"I guess I do try to make people happy," she was saying softly. "It isn't that hard and it's ever so much nicer than making them sad, don't you think?"

"I can't say that I've ever thought about it quite that way. Normally what I do doesn't make the people I deal with happy at all."

"Weren't the people at the restaurant happy when you caught those robbers?"

"Yes, but the robbers weren't."

"Did they need the money? I mean did they have families, children who were hungry? Why did they rob the restaurant?"

"To get money for drugs."

"Then they deserved to be unhappy. I wouldn't worry about it. Are you ready to eat now?"

"Yes, I think we'd better."

They ate scrambled eggs and limp toast, drank hot sweet coffee, and watched the sun burst over the trees and light up the mid-morning sky through Sarah's hayloft window.

Asa Canyon learned about Sarah's father and how he'd died, slowly and painfully over a long period. But Sarah didn't remember it with sadness. Their relationship seemed filled with joy that overshadowed the bad times. He picked up the hesitation in her voice when she described her mother and her remarriage two years ago.

In time he stopped trying to make order out

of Sarah's conversation. When she explained that she normally closed her shop on Saturday and that she didn't open it again until she felt like it, he didn't argue. He didn't understand people who ran their lives like that, but the late summer morning was too golden, and Sarah's brown eyes too caring to allow any further discord. Afterwards they washed the dishes and put them away. He'd delayed his departure as long as he legitimately could when he finally stood up and cleared his throat.

"Sarah, I appreciate what you did for me last night, the way you tried to make me feel better about what happened. Nobody has ever cared much about my feelings and I thank you. Now, I'd better get back to town. I ought to check in with my office and report my truck as stolen."

"No, don't go, Deputy Canyon. I assume you must be off today, since you haven't said anything about being late for work."

"Well, I did sign out for today and tomorrow, since I expected Jeanie to be here."

"Of course. Naturally, you'd expect to be . . . with her."

"Sarah, you don't understand," Asa began. "The truth is there really wasn't anything like that between us."

"You don't have to explain, Asa Canyon. All I need is to be with you, even just for today."

"Sarah, I don't think you know what you're saying. I mean you saw what happened when

I kissed you. Being with me would not be wise."

"Oh, I don't know about that. But if it makes you uncomfortable, we'll explore other ways to release your tension."

Asa groaned. Exploring with Sarah was the primary cause of his tension. He didn't think that he could take much more.

"I'm afraid to ask what you have in mind?"

"Softball."

"Softball? Sarah, I'm not very good at playing ball."

"That's okay. My team just plays for fun. We'll find something for you to do. Do you have a glove?"

"Not since I was in high school. If I remember right my glove was retired during my junior year by request from the rest of the team."

"Well, no matter. I have an extra one, and a shirt and running shoes, too. Let me change clothes, and we'll see what we can do," she said. "Wait here."

Uneasy, Asa watched Sarah dance out of the kitchen and down the corridor. He was lousy at certain sports. Golf, hunting, and fishing, he'd mastered. But football, basketball, and baseball always made him feel like a stick figure dancing on a hand-held board. In everything else he'd played, he'd been all knees and feet.

Before he could begin to formulate a refusal Sarah was back and he lost every rational thought he might have voiced. She was wearing a pair of shorts and another T-shirt. This one said, "Smyrna Smart Guys" on the front, and had the number 32 on the back. He didn't know anything about the guys on her team, but if they were anything like the women, the opponents might as well give up.

Sarah handed him a matching shirt, a pair of running shoes, and a glove. "I think you can wear this glove. It belonged to one of our guys who broke his ankle. There's an extra cap in the van and a couple of bats. I hope the shoes fit. They belonged to my dad. Fortunately, you don't have to have cleats. We don't take this very seriously."

Asa glanced at his watch. "Isn't this early for a ball game? Even the chickens don't get started before noon."

"We're playing in the end-of-the-year tournament. The league winner goes to the state finals. They've already been playing for hours."

"And I can just come in and play without having been a member of the team?"

"Yep. We're allowed to add three people to the roster for the grand finale."

Oh, great, he was part of the grand finale, substituting for a player who'd broken an ankle. Somehow that seemed to be an omen. Until he looked at Sarah's confident expression and felt her smile melt all his hesitation.

Officer Paul Martin was the Smyrna Smart Guys' pitcher. Asa recognized Jake Dalton, the young mayor of Smyrna, as the catcher. Sarah played shortstop and more or less directed everyone. Two other women and seven men completed the mixed roster. They welcomed Asa and after a few warm-up tosses, the game got underway.

Though it had been years since he'd been on a field, Asa gave it his best. After he endured two strikeouts and missed three fly balls in a row, Sarah took pity on him and suggested he keep score and man the water buckets. Asa agreed with gratitude. Someone called his name. He looked up and nodded at a fellow county police officer who wandered up.

"Canyon, didn't know you were playing on Sarah's team."

Damn. He'd hoped that nobody would recognize him. "Neither did I," Asa said with a warning in his voice. "It just happened."

"Yeah, Sarah's hard to turn down. She's a good person, Canyon," he said, and wandered off.

Hard to turn down? Watching Sarah's long legs as she ran across the infield and scooped up a ground ball made Asa uncomfortably aware of what playing with Sarah could mean. Like some teenager with a crush, he studied her, fighting the threat of an erection with every move she made.

At one point when the Smart Guys were up to bat, Sarah glanced at her watch, came over, gave him a hug, and asked, "You okay?"

"Sure. Why?"

She didn't answer. She just smiled and took the field after the third out. It took Asa a few minutes to figure out that Sarah had just wanted to make him feel better. And he did. At least he felt something that promised infinite possibilities. That is, if he was into promises.

A moment later, when Asa noticed that the right fielder was playing too deep, he yelled, "Move in, move in."

The batter made Asa's call look good by dropping a soft fly ball just over the first baseman's head. When the outfielder made the catch, Sarah gave Asa a thumbs-up sign. By the next inning, Asa was moving the players around the field as if he'd been appointed coach and they were playing the World Series.

It wasn't until Sarah came and sat down beside him that he realized she was distressed.

"What's wrong, Sarah? We're winning."

"Yep, but the guys aren't accustomed to being managed by someone so serious about winning. They just like to fool around, do their own thing, you know? No pressure. Relax."

"But you're good, really good. Don't you want to win? These guys you're playing signal what they're going to do. Why not take advantage of it?"

"Because that makes it too serious, Asa. I tell the others what to do sometimes, but this is mostly just for fun. If we miss a ball, we don't care. If they hit it over our heads, fine. We'll get it next time."

Asa bit back a retort. She was serious. They didn't care whether they won or not. Twice Jake Dalton sat down and watched the ball bounce around behind him while he laughed at his own lack of skill. With a little organization Sarah's team could probably beat any of the teams he saw playing, but they'd rather goof off. He continued to keep the score book, but the game lost some of its interest for him.

The Smart Guys managed to pull out a win in the seventh inning. Afterward, Asa found himself swept up in the group going for pizza. By the time they'd finished eating and celebrating it was midafternoon. He hadn't checked in with his office and he still hadn't reported the theft of his truck. He didn't know how he felt about the day. He couldn't quite remember ever spending one like it. He'd certainly never met a woman like Sarah before.

Now they were in her van with Mayor Dalton, who'd bummed a ride. Sarah was singing rowdily.

"Come on, Asa," Jake cajoled. "How can we sing rounds with only two people?"

"What in hell are rounds?"

He hadn't intended to sound so gruff. He was beginning to feel out of sorts again and he didn't know why. There was no reason for him to be angry at Jake, except it was obvious that the mayor was Sarah's friend and that he'd like to be more. Asa had no claims on Sarah, even if he had kissed her. Even if she had kissed him back. Even if her face had a smudge of red dirt across her forehead that he wanted to wipe away. This was her van and he was the guest.

"Rounds," Sarah explained politely, "are when we each sing the same song at different times. I start with *Row, row, row your boat*. When I get to the second line, Jake comes in. When he gets to the second line, you come in."

"Forget it," Asa growled. "I don't sing any better than I bat."

Sarah looked over at Jake and said, "You have to forgive him, Jake. Today was very hard for him. He doesn't mean to be a grouch."

"Oh? How's that?" Jake asked innocently.

"Asa had—"

"His truck stolen," Asa said sharply.

"Sorry," Jake sympathized. "I can't believe a thief would steal a deputy sheriff's truck. Obviously he didn't know whose vehicle it was."

"The thief knew."

"Well, if it took place in Smyrna, I'm sure our fine police department will apprehend the culprit in no time," Jake offered. "Don't suppose you'd like to swap over from county to city law enforcement, would you?"

"Nope. Nothing personal, mayor, but living in the city drives me crazy. I like my privacy and my log cabin too much. I don't know how you fellows stand it."

"Speaking as mayor, I disagree. But I'm afraid that Sarah prefers the country, too. You ought to get her to show you her playhouse sometime. We had some fine times there when we were teenagers."

Sarah and the mayor? In her barn? "I'll bet you did." The idea of Sarah comforting someone else suddenly made Asa angry. "Let me off here," he blurted out. "I think I'll run the rest of the way to Jeanie's apartment. I have to see the manager about breaking the lease and returning that bed."

Sarah reluctantly pulled over. Of course he didn't want to go home. She didn't want him to. She could even understand that he was delaying, but she'd gone as far as she could to keep him from being alone without being pushy. "Are you sure?"

"I'm sure."

"Well, all right. But how will you get from the apartment to your cabin?"

"I'll call for a county car from the apartment manager's office. Don't worry. This will give me time to work through my thoughts. Besides, exercise is good for the body I was told," Asa added, pointedly looking at Sarah.

Sarah flushed. "Good. I've always said, physical expression of emotion is always the best release."

"Sure," Asa said as he got out of the van. "But there are better ways than running."

"Yeah," Jake agreed with a warning smile as Asa slammed the door. "A cold shower. Bye, Asa. Our next game is tomorrow morning, if you want to give it another try."

"No thanks, I think a cold shower is easier on the nerves."

Sarah watched the sharp interchange between Jake and Asa in confusion. She didn't know what set Jake off. He was normally congenial and fun. She didn't think that Asa could ever be thought of in those terms. But there were other ways to judge a man.

She watched Asa lope down the sidewalk, his long legs and arms moving in a measured rhythm. Organized, even down to his jogging, Sarah observed.

Asa might think that he was working off his tension, but watching him run she wasn't sure that he knew how. Every step he took was like another line on her drawing. His trek was turning into a muddle. By the time he got to the apartment, he would have worried his mind into a frazzle.

Sarah released the clutch and pressed the gas pedal. Asa Canyon was definitely a Type A personality—go, go, go, full speed ahead. He needed to slow down and smell the flowers. It looked as if she'd have to teach him how. Asa Canyon was a caring man and maybe, just maybe he'd let her show him what it meant to be cared for in return.

She'd already found a way to reach him, with a kiss. No matter how much he protested, he liked kissing her. His body told her the truth, even if he tried to pretend otherwise.

Sarah didn't think that she was in love with Deputy Canyon. Love didn't develop that quickly, but there was something between them. She was beginning to suspect that there were man/woman relationships that she didn't understand. Still, her kiss was a promise, a promise to find out.

"Where is Asa's cabin, Jake?" she asked casually.

"Out by the lake."

"I didn't know there was a cabin there."

"Most folks don't. You have to cut down past the lake and around behind the dam."

Sarah's only comment was "Hmm."

When she stopped at the mayor's house to let him out, Jake surprised her by reaching over and taking her face in his hands. He touched his lips to hers and said, "That's just to say that I like you, Sarah Wilson."

"You do?"

"I do, and I don't want the deputy to cut me out without you knowing it."

"The deputy is only interested in his job, Jake. He's just being a . . . a—"

"Don't say friend, Sarah. Asa Canyon may be many things, but I don't think a friend is one of them. Everybody in law enforcement knew about him long before he left his security job and came to Cobb County. He's a legend, and he's hard. Be careful. He's known to be pretty single-minded when he's after something."

"Why are you telling me this?"

"Because whether you know it or not, I think the deputy's after you."

All the way down Atlanta Road toward her shop Sarah thought about Jake's statement. In spite of what Jake said, she knew Asa

Canyon wasn't the kind of man who flitted from woman to woman like a hummingbird. Asa Canyon didn't have casual flings. Whatever he did, he went all out.

Still, Jake Dalton was a pretty smart man. If he thought that Asa was interested, who was she to argue? Maybe he wasn't a ballplayer, but the man definitely had other talents. She'd just have to teach him that it wasn't winning that mattered, but the friendship that they enjoyed. Sarah smiled. What was friendlier than kissing?

Sarah checked the mailbox in her shop. Nothing but a few bills, which she jammed into the box beneath the counter that she used as a cash drawer. She was about to leave when a taxi stopped in front and an elderly man got out. He stopped and took a long look around before he came inside.

"Excuse me," he said, hesitating as he gave Sarah a curious look and took another furtive glance around. "Is the locksmith in?"

"I'm the locksmith," Sarah explained. "I know I don't look like it, but I've been playing in a softball tournament."

"You? Is there anyone else here?"

"No, just me." Then she remembered Asa's warning about risky situations. "I mean not at the moment, but I expect the men to be back shortly."

"I have a job for you."

Sarah watched the man return to the cab. He and the driver brought a small lead safe inside and placed it on the counter. As the taxi drove away, Sarah's customer counted his change and placed it in a purse made of leather and strung together with thongs, the kind that a child might make in a craft class at summer camp. He was having a hard time holding it because the thumb on his right hand was missing. It looked as if it hadn't been gone long.

"Can you open this?" He cocked his head toward the safe. "Without destroying it?"

"Probably. What is it?"

The man was pale. Either he hadn't been in the sun much, or had been ill. He kept glancing at his watch and at the street outside as if he was expecting someone.

Finally he raised his eyes and stared at her. "It's a safe, an old safe that came out of my family's home. The house is being renovated. The safe was . . . discovered during the reconstruction. It dates back to the mid-eighteen-hundreds. Have you ever seen one like it before?"

"No, I don't think so. Is your house around here?"

"Yes."

Sarah considered his story. The only house in the city of Smyrna that was being renovated was the old Grimsley house, which lay in the middle of the new Smyrna Village project. Jake and the city council had decided to incorporate the Grimsley house, along with the recently refurbished Bank of Smyrna building, into the Village.

"You mean the Grimsley house?"

He looked startled. "Yes, do you know it?"

"Sure, everybody does. The house escaped being burned by Sherman because the first Miss Lois sat on the front porch with an ax and threatened to cut off the head of the first man to reach the steps. Her namesake taught most of us in first grade at FitzHugh Lee Grammar School. She died last year. I didn't know that there were any relatives."

"Yes, I'm Miss Lois's great-nephew. I . . . I was away. I only just found out about the project. Of course I don't own the house. Miss Lois left it to the city. But I'd heard about it all my life and I . . . I had permission to look around before they began the restoration."

He held out the hand with no thumb. "My name is Lincoln Grimsley."

Sarah shook it.

She studied the safe. It was very old, the custom-built kind. The lock was a series of irregularly shaped squares with worn numbers on the surface. It was unlike anything Sarah had ever seen. From the look of it, short of blowing it up with explosives, the only way she'd get it open was by trial and error.

"Have you tried to open it?"

"Yes. I took it to two other locksmiths first. They finally said that the only way we could open it was to blow it up. But because it's so small, explosives might destroy it. I'd rather not do that."

"What's in it?" Sarah asked, trying to be as efficient in her approach as possible.

"Well, I'm not certain but, according to my

grandfather, the safe was hidden during the Civil War. It was never found—until now. The safe was to be inherited by the oldest male child. But nobody knew where it was."

"How'd you find it?"

"I've been staying in the house for the last week. When the workers began their renovation they found a room that had been sealed off. I was able to find the safe hidden there."

"Does the city know you have it?"

"No," Lincoln admitted. "Please, don't tell them. It isn't that I mind their knowing. Legally the safe is mine. It's just that it wouldn't be safe for this information to become public knowledge."

"It wouldn't?"

"Please, ma'am. I'll go to the authorities when the safe is open. I promise. First I need to know what's inside. It's very important."

Along with being tired and shaky, the old man seemed desperate.

"It isn't anything dangerous," he promised. "In fact there may be nothing at all inside. It isn't heavy enough to contain gold or silver. The story I was told was that the safe contains a great deal of money, hidden there during the war. I'm guessing that if that's true, the money will be Confederate and therefore worthless. It's just that I only have a week to—I mean I have an appointment next week and I need to know. Could you hurry, please?"

"Look, Mr. Grimsley. There's no way I can possibly open this safe in a few minutes. I'll have to study it. It may take days, even weeks."

He looked stricken. "I'd hoped to have it open by tomorrow. Couldn't you try?"

Sarah looked at her watch. It was late and she was tired. She wanted nothing more than to get home and think about what had happened in the last eighteen hours. Still, she couldn't just walk away and leave the old man. It was obvious that he was worried.

"I tell you what. Let me take it home and work on it the rest of the weekend."

"Take it home? I'd hoped to keep this confidential. I'd planned to stay with you as you worked on it."

"I'm sorry, Mr. Grimsley, but I have no way of knowing how long it will take. I promise you, it will be safer with me than here in the shop. I'm personal friends with the deputy sheriff," she said, trying to reassure him.

"Sheriff?" This time there was no mistaking his distress. "Oh, but—" Then he seemed to resign himself to her plan. "Well, I guess I don't have any choice. You're my last hope. And maybe it would be safer there."

Sarah bent down and lifted the safe. Lincoln Grimsley was right. It wasn't that heavy. After she got the safe into the back of the van, they returned to the shop. He promised to check back in the morning to see whether Sarah had been successful.

"You'll keep this confidential, won't you, Miss Wilson?"

"I promise. If you're worried, I could give you a claim ticket."

He started. "Oh, no, that won't be necessary. But if you do get it open, you won't disturb the contents, will you? I mean I can trust you to leave everything just as you found it?"

"Certainly."

But that didn't seem to satisfy the man. In fact he was becoming even more agitated. "Your friend, the sheriff, won't bother it?"

"Of course not. Who sent you to me, Mr. Grimsley?"

"A police officer down at City Hall, an Officer Martin, who let me into the house. He said that I could trust you completely."

"Give me until Monday, Mr. Grimsley, and I'll see what I can do. Otherwise, you're welcome to take the safe back with you."

"No. That wouldn't be a good idea. I'll leave it."

"Can I drop you somewhere?" Sarah asked in an attempt to coax him out the door.

"No thanks." He peered once more out the window, then quickly slipped out. By the time Sarah had pulled the blinds, turned off the lights, and locked up, he was gone. She didn't know how he could have disappeared so quickly. She didn't even know how to reach him.

Sarah shook her head. There were a lot of strange people in the world, and locksmiths ran into many of them. But Miss Lois's great-nephew? Sarah found it odd that she'd never heard him mentioned before. Older people often rattled off their family history at the drop of a hat.

But apparently he'd checked with City Hall for permission to enter the house. They wouldn't have let him inside if he wasn't who he said he was. Anyway, if Paul had sent him over, he had to be all right.

It was getting late. She was tired and dirty. No wonder the old man had asked if there was someone else around. If she'd come into the shop she wouldn't believe that she was a locksmith either. As she drove away, Sarah tried to concentrate on the safe in the back. She couldn't. All she could think about was a stern, lean figure who loped in measured strides.

When she reached the barn Sarah backed the van directly below the hayloft. She ran upstairs, opened the second-floor doors, and lowered the old iron grate she and her father had fashioned into a dumbwaiter for lifting equipment. Later, when Sarah had turned the loft into her living quarters, she'd been grateful for the setup. With it, she'd been able to pull building supplies and furniture up to the second floor.

With a little effort she rolled the small safe out of the van and onto the grate. By using a system of pulleys she raised the grate up to the hayloft doors, then ran back upstairs and pulled it, and the safe, inside.

She'd have a look at the safe as soon as she was relaxed enough to concentrate. First she drank a glass of iced tea. Several minutes later, she made a peanut butter and jelly sandwich and poured herself a glass of milk. Nothing satisfied her.

By midnight she'd given up on the safe and was pacing the floor while carrying on a debate with herself. Asa Canyon might be accustomed to being by himself, but he didn't like it. He'd lost someone he cared about and she knew how that felt. And he ought not to be alone now.

Sarah reached into her closet and pulled out the first thing she touched, a deep rose sundress with slim ribbon straps. She stepped into a pair of white sandals and dashed down the stairs. Besides, she couldn't be mistaken about the way he'd responded to her kiss.

No, Asa Canyon shouldn't be alone. And he wouldn't be, if Sarah could help it. A kiss was a promise, and if she was right, Asa would welcome her. If she was wrong, she'd turn around and come home and nobody would know but her.

Four

Across the lake the moon hung low over the
stand of loblolly pines. Asa studied the golden
reflection on the water and decided that it
looked like a spaceship, its exhaust wavering
outward where the water rippled against the
shore. The spaceship made him think of Sarah.

Everything made him think of Sarah.

He stood in the doorway listening to the
silence, restless, unable to settle down, waiting for something he couldn't explain.

A layer of fog began to roll in over the
surface of the water as the night air cooled. A
frog's voice pierced the air exploding like the
urgent siren of an emergency vehicle on a
rescue mission.

The phone rang. It was Jeanie.

Apologetic, anxious, at the same time un-
deniably happy, she wanted Asa to know that

she and Mike were married. They were truly in love, perfect together. Mike loved to travel and he could go with her, wherever her assignments led her. She hadn't known what Mike had done until they were on the plane. She hoped that Asa wouldn't hate her for loving Mike.

"I won't, not if you really love him," Asa said. "But you tell that smart aleck you ran off with that I'm planning his torture. He can just get ready."

Mike came on the phone. "I wouldn't have done it, old buddy, if you'd understood. But you weren't about to, and we didn't have time for you to come around, so I had no choice."

In the end Asa gave them his blessings. He wondered, after the connection had been broken, if he would have been so willing to wish them well if it weren't for Sarah.

When he answered the knock on the door a moment later and found her standing there, he wasn't sure whether she was real or he was hallucinating.

Then she threw her arms around his neck and for a moment he gave in to the feeling of contentment she brought with her. Until he realized that what she was giving was more than comfort, and that he had no right to it.

"You and the mayor were both wrong," he said tightly. "Running doesn't work, and cold showers only give me goose bumps."

"I know," she responded softly. "Neither does peanut better and jelly. That's why I came back."

"Maybe we'd better talk about this."

"Must we? I'd rather you kiss me."

"Sarah, I don't think what you're asking for is that simple. Let me put on my pants and we'll go for a walk."

"Put on your pants?"

Asa turned back into the dark cabin.

Sarah followed.

He stepped into a room off the small living area and turned on the light. Through the crack in the door Sarah could see him clearly. Tonight his underwear was blue. He stepped into a pair of faded worn jeans and picked up a pair of sneakers.

She blushed and walked over to the window overlooking the lake. Waiting for him to dress, she sat on the sill in the moonlight.

"Deputy Canyon?"

He tied the last shoelace and slid his arms into the sleeves of a knit shirt, pulling it over his head as he joined her. "I think we're past Deputy Canyon and Ms. Wilson, Sarah. My name is Asa."

She looked up at him, her face showing a spark of humor. "All right, Asa. I just wanted to point out that nobody is watching now. This isn't in the line of duty."

"It isn't?"

"It isn't." She kissed him.

He knew he shouldn't let it happen. Last night's first kiss had been a necessary ploy. The second, an accident.

He groaned.

This kiss was a crazy wonderful mistake

and he gave in to it with full cooperation and little thought of where it might lead. He had a sudden vision of a beach, a hot summer night, and two lovers, linked together on the sand by some secluded lagoon. The sound of a water creature breaking the surface and falling back into the darkness gave way to the call of a night bird in the distance. It all seemed part of the moment, tied with the touch and feel of the woman in his arms.

It was the blowing of a car horn that finally broke through his rapture and interrupted their embrace. Asa walked out onto the porch, giving silent thanks to Officer Paul Martin, who was driving up behind Sarah's van. Behind Paul was Asa's silver truck, being driven by another blue-uniformed officer.

"Believe it or not," Paul called out, "we found your truck parked in the mayor's space at City Hall. There was a pile of clothes on the seat and a note that said the keys and your gun were under the mat and would we please deliver them to you. So, here we are."

"City Hall." Asa scowled. "That figures. Mike wouldn't dare leave Silver Girl some place where she would be stolen. Thanks, Martin. I owe you one."

The driver of the truck pulled into the space at the corner of the house, slid out, and climbed into the patrol car. Without a comment on the late hour, or Sarah's presence, Paul gave a thumbs-up salute and drove away.

Asa looked down at Sarah and realized that her very presence here linked them together, whether or not he wanted it. She'd rescued him, handed over the keys to her van, and made him a part of her softball team, all of which tied them to each other. He worried that even though Smyrna hugged the perimeter of Atlanta, it was still a small town at heart. Members of the inner circle, those whose parents and grandparents had been born here, were still protective of their own. And Sarah was one of theirs.

He caught her hand. "Let's go for a walk before I do something to get myself arrested. Deputies aren't immune from the wrath of a man who believes he's protecting a woman."

"Who? Paul Martin?" Sarah asked, putting her arm around Asa's waist as they walked across the yard. "He's just a friend."

"I was thinking more about the mayor." They wandered over to the lake and followed a well-worn path around the moonlit water.

"Jake Dalton is a friend, too."

"I don't think that's his choice."

"How old are you, Asa?"

"I'm thirty-five, old enough to know better than to let you make yourself a part of my life under false pretenses."

"Good. I like a man who knows what he's doing, especially when what he's doing feels so good."

"Oh, lady," he said under his breath, "I think the deputy sheriff is in big trouble."

Asa didn't know how to respond to Sarah's honesty. She thought he needed her and she came. He knew that he could invite her inside the cabin and she wouldn't hesitate, but that would take them one step further in a direction that he wasn't sure he was ready to go.

Asa removed her arm from his waist and held her hand, his long fingers loosely threaded through her shorter ones.

"Sarah, Jeanie called tonight, before you came. I gave her and Mike my blessings."

"I'm glad."

Asa stopped and turned to study Sarah in the moonlight.

"Why did you really come here tonight?" he asked.

"Because I didn't want you to be alone."

He gave a dry laugh. "You didn't have to bother. I'm an expert at being alone. I ought to be, I've had a lot of experience with it."

"I don't understand, Asa." She caught his arm. "Tell me why you're alone."

"All right," he finally said. "I was brought up in an orphanage, a real orphanage, Sarah. I don't even know who my parents were. I was the kid everybody took home and returned. As soon as I graduated from high school I joined the Marines. From then on, it was me who was leaving."

"You've never had anybody?"

"I guess Jeanie is the only family I've ever had."

"Oh, Asa, I'm so sorry they didn't love you. You must have been very strong to survive."

"Don't feel sorry for me. I wasn't a nice child. But one thing I finally learned is that a man is responsible for making himself happy. He can't depend on anyone else. People are temporary. They can be replaced."

Asa was talking to Sarah, but he was also talking to himself, working through the problem, just as he always did until he had an answer that he could deal with.

People are temporary? Sarah couldn't even begin to argue with his calm acceptance of loss.

"Believe me, Sarah, for a time, Jeanie thought that she wanted the security I offered. She needed to feel wanted, to have someone care about her. Now, she has Mike. And that's good."

"You truly aren't grieving?"

"I'm not grieving."

With her free hand Sarah reached up and touched Asa's face. "If you don't want me here, I'd better go. I don't know how to be temporary."

Asa looked down at her stricken expression. He was rejecting what she was offering, and she didn't know how to deal with it.

"Yes, you'd better, Sarah. For if you stay I'll only mess up your life."

"I don't believe that."

"You should. I'm not kind and giving. And I don't know how to accept your compassion."

"That's not true, Asa. You care about people. That makes you special in my book."

"Not people. Just Jeanie and she was a responsibility, like my job. Being with you isn't the same."

"It isn't? I'm glad."

He drew Sarah's hand to his mouth, where he planted a quick kiss on her palm, then let go.

"Ah hell, Sarah, go home while I can still let you go. This can't work. I'd make you miserable."

"Why don't you let me decide?"

"I'm compulsively neat," he went on, as if he was trying to convince himself as well as Sarah. "My bathroom doesn't have any extra toothbrushes in the cabinet because I don't like people in my house. My truck sits too high off the ground for a lady to climb in and out of because I don't welcome a woman's company. In other words, I'm a man who has a plan for every part of his life, and you're a lady—"

"Without one," she finished. "Maybe you're right. But I think you may be wrong about what a man has to do to be happy. Maybe there are times when it's better to forget all your plans and fly blind into the sun."

She couldn't read the expression in his eyes in the darkness. But she could feel the tension in his touch. He should have loosened his grip and stepped back if he wanted her to believe that he was pulling away. But he didn't. Instead there was an almost imperceptible movement that brought him even closer.

Sarah's heart was thudding in her chest. Her knees felt shaky.

"I'm sorry, Asa. I don't seem to be very smart about this. I feel wicked for even thinking it. I guess I'm not a truly noble person. I'm not even being honest about why I'm here. The real reason I came"—her voice dropped into a throaty whisper—"is because I think that I want *you.*"

"That's crazy," he said.

"I know, but it's true."

In the darkness, Sarah felt the erratic rhythm of her heartbeat. She could hear Asa's breathing as his chest' expanded and compressed. He wasn't any more controlled than she.

A long moment passed before he spoke. "Are you sure you want to take a chance on getting involved with a man like me?"

Sarah closed her eyes for a moment and tried to think logically about her reply. But she couldn't. She kept remembering her father's belief that a person had only one shot at the brass ring and he had to go for it, or forever regret the loss. Her father never considered not playing ball, even though his playing hastened his death. The only thing he ever talked about was the great joy his life had brought to him.

There was no logic to her feelings for Asa Canyon, or to her actions. All she was certain of was that Asa refused to let himself hold her when his need to do so was as great as hers.

"Do I want to get involved with you? I already am," she said, and was rewarded with a groan of desperation as his arms locked around her. Their lips met and fused. His kiss was wild and hard as he nibbled his way across her face, pulling on her lips, her cheeks, her ears, as if she were an oasis offering water to a man dying of thirst. There was nothing gentle about him, or about his touch.

There was nothing tentative about her offering herself to him. She tilted her head to reach his mouth and curved her body to give him the freedom to reach her.

The night went quiet. Even the frog across the lake had fallen silent—until a response came from another web-footed creature. Their baroque mating call startled Asa, drawing him back to the present. He slowly brought his kisses to a stop.

Dazed, Sarah pulled back and stared at Asa.

"My, my," she whispered. "When you do something, you go all out, don't you?"

"I tried to tell you, Sarah. In another minute I'd have had you on the ground and you know what I would have wanted."

"I think I do," she said softly. "But I'm not sure that I'm ready for that—not yet."

"I'm damn sure you're not," he said, his voice sharp with barely controlled fury. "That's why you're going to get into Henry and go home now!"

"All right, if that's what you want."

"You know damn well that's not what I want. But what I've already taken is all I'm going to get."

Asa put his hand on her shoulder and directed her back toward the cabin. He put Sarah in the van and slammed the door.

"Go home, Sarah. Call me when you get there."

"I don't have your number," she managed to say, forcing the words past the lump that had almost closed off her throat.

"I'll get it."

From the wallet he found under the seat in his truck, he extracted a business card, and with a pen, jotted his private number on the back. When he handed it to Sarah he made certain that their hands didn't touch.

"Call me," he directed, "as soon as you get there, so I won't worry."

"Thank you, Asa. I like thinking that you would worry about me."

She called twenty minutes later. When he heard her voice he didn't trust himself to say more than "Fine."

Sarah didn't try to force the conversation. For now, that was enough.

Asa Canyon raised his arm, took aim, and pulled the trigger four times. The result was one shot in the heart of the cardboard bank robber, two in his arm, and one—who knew where. He'd been firing his gun for the better part of an hour, a task that he normally found soothing. The weapons range usually put things in proper perspective for him. Today he found his mind wandering. Today he was drawing a crowd of onlookers, not from his sharpshooting, but from his misses.

With a groan he tore the goggles and ear

protectors from his face and left the sound-proof room. He might as well quit. He was only wasting bullets.

He'd spent Sunday morning running around the lake and reading the newspaper, and the afternoon catching up on his paperwork. The firing range had killed another hour. A quick supper at Speedy's Grill had carried him to nine o'clock. So far he'd managed to put Sarah Wilson and the ball tournament out of his mind.

As he left the building he came to a stop, made a circle, and went back inside to the lockup room where Clarence was grumbling louder than usual as he filled out a form.

"Clarence?"

"Yeah, man, what you need? If it's a report, or a file, forget it. I won't be caught up here before Christmas and it ain't even Halloween."

"Relax, buddy, all I want is some information."

"Yeah, what?"

"You know anything about the locksmiths in this county? I mean I busted my cuffs and I want to find somebody to take a look at them."

"Well, there's Jimmy J. over on Roswell Road."

"No, I mean—I heard that there's a woman who's pretty good."

He'd thought he was being casual, but from the quick jerk of Clarence's head Asa knew that he hadn't fooled him at all.

"Sarah, huh? That'd be Sarah Wilson. Everybody knows Sarah. Her daddy, Big Jim Wilson, was one of the best catchers the Atlanta Crackers ever had."

Asa didn't recognize the name, but he'd heard some of the men over at the courthouse talk about Atlanta's Triple A team and Jim Wilson, the man with the big heart. He'd played hurt for the last two years of his career. When he'd finally hung it up, he'd still been a young man, but with a body that was broken and maimed. But locksmith? Canyon was surprised.

"Where is her place?"

"In Oakdale, between South Cobb and Atlanta Road. You can't miss it."

Asa knew the area. He told himself that he wasn't going over there. Sarah was too young for him. She was too fresh and innocent for him. She was too giving for her own good. He had to protect her from herself. But he didn't listen.

Sarah's building was dilapidated and in need of fresh paint. The Wilson's Lock Service sign was almost unreadable. Leaving his truck running, Asa got out and stepped up to the shop. Resting against the window was a message printed on a piece of cardboard:

PLAYING IN A TOURNAMENT TODAY. OPEN MONDAY ABOUT 10:00, PROBABLY. SARAH.

He hadn't expected her to be open on Sunday, but certainly on Monday. *Open about*

10:00, probably? What kind of business did she run? No regular hours. Midnight calls to a location she didn't know, to unlock the handcuffs on a man chained to a brass bed. What kind of risks did she routinely take? He bet she didn't even have an answering service that kept up with her calls.

A quick stop at a phone booth proved how right his guess was. An answering machine crackled on and Sarah's cheerful voice chimed out, "Hi, this is Sarah. I'm at the ball park. Be back sooner or later. If this is Mother, the money for the electric company is under the mat. If it's anybody else, don't you dare touch it. Bye now. Oh, yes, if this happens to be Asa, the coffee pot's on the stove if you want to come by later. I'll be alone and in need of company."

Asa swore.

The money's under the mat.

I'll be alone and in need of company.

Sarah Wilson was practically inviting anyone who called her number to rob her. Asa cringed.

At least she hadn't given out her address. Anybody who took advantage of her open invitation would either have to know where Sarah lived or look up her address, which was—he flipped through the directory—listed right there under her name.

Being trusting was one thing, but being foolish was something that Asa Canyon couldn't tolerate. He'd learned that the hard way. He told himself it was his sense of responsibility that made him slam the phone book closed and burn rubber as he roared off down the highway.

Twenty minutes later he was knocking on Sarah's barn door. The loading door to the hayloft creaked open and Sarah looked down.

"Come on up. The outside door's open."

"Of course it is," he grumbled under his breath as he climbed the steps. "Why?" he asked as she opened the door to her living quarters. "Why would you leave such a message on your answering machine? Suppose somebody other than me called you?"

"Suppose they did? If their name isn't Asa, they aren't invited. The coffee's hot."

Open-mouthed, Asa just stood there. He was so stunned that he could neither move nor answer her. Sarah must have been in bed, reading—with the door open.

She had a pair of eyeglasses with red frames shoved back on her head, holding her boyish hair away from her face. She was wearing an oversize white T-shirt with a seashell and the name "Jekyll Island" spelled out across her breasts. The bottom of the shirt hit her thighs about halfway to her knees. Her feet were bare. She looked so desirable, and he wanted to smother her in his arms.

"Do you have an oilcan?" he said, cursing himself for not having a reasonable argument against what she thought was a reasonable statement.

"An oilcan? Why, are we playing Wizard of Oz?"

"We're not playing anything."

"Are you angry with me, Asa?"

"Yes! No! I don't know what I am."

Asa felt his frustration tighten into a knot somewhere between his belly button and his—damn! He couldn't even let himself think about that part of his body. He knew that he was cutting her into pieces with his gaze. His rigid control was in shambles, all because he wanted to kiss her so badly that it frightened him.

Sarah met his frown with a smile. "Don't worry, Asa. I know you're worried about me. You wouldn't be yelling if you weren't. I forgive you. Come inside and close the door. I think there's an oilcan around here somewhere."

Once he was inside, she raised her hand and placed one finger against his lips as if she were imploring him to put his anger away. And somehow the gesture worked. Her touch seemed to calm the anger that raged through him.

"Your outside door to the hayloft squeaks," he said at last. "I'll oil it for you."

"It does? I hadn't noticed."

"I know. You never see a problem, do you?"

"Not if I can help it." Sarah was now on her knees in front of the cabinet beneath the sink, pulling out an assortment of cleaning supplies and cooking utensils. "I know it's in here someplace."

Asa squatted down beside her, choking back a reprimand. "You keep all this stuff in here together?"

"Sure. I don't use these pans much so it doesn't matter if I can't get to them easily. Nope, not here. Maybe it's mixed in with the canned goods."

"But, Sarah, all the cleaning supplies should be in one place. Pots and pans should be in one place, and food—"

"Oh, yes, I remember," she interrupted. "It's in the van in my tool kit. I'll be right back."

Asa automatically began replacing the items in the cabinet in an orderly manner. By the time Sarah returned he had organized the two adjacent cabinets, using every available space.

"My, my, that's really neat," she commented, handing Asa the can of oil. "Do you do windows?" she asked as he greased the noisy hinges.

"Every March."

Sarah folded her arms across her chest and rocked back and forth on the balls of her feet. "And you're kind to women and children. You have the oil in your truck changed every 3,000 miles, and I'll bet you never tear the label off a pillow, do you?"

Asa was having trouble focusing on her question. Her folded arms lifted her breasts enticingly. She wasn't wearing a bra, and he couldn't keep himself from staring.

"I've never met anyone as innocent as you, Sarah," Asa said in a gravelly voice. "You seem to have appointed yourself my guardian angel and I don't know what to do about it. When I opened that door last night and you were standing there you turned me to butter and I haven't been worth a damn since and I don't like that."

"I know."

"How do you know? What makes you so smart, lady?"

"Because I feel the same way. The only difference is, I've decided not to fight it."

"And that's what I don't understand. Why?"

"Come over to the table and sit down." Sarah held out her hand. Asa took it.

Together they walked over to the little table by the window that overlooked the pasture beyond. Asa let go of Sarah and forced himself to sit down across from her. He ought to get out of there. She wasn't part of his future, and he knew it. But, damn it, he wanted her like he'd never wanted anyone before.

Sarah filled their cups with coffee. She could sense the battle raging inside Asa. She needed to put some space between them, to give him time to find his way. If there was one thing she'd learned about Asa Canyon, it was that he needed his time to work through a problem. She sat down, pulled her chair to the table and folded her hands beneath her chin.

"My father was a baseball player," she began.

"I know. Big Jim Wilson, with the Atlanta Crackers. Hit twenty-four home runs in his last season."

"He'd known for a long time that his knees were going. He'd already lost hearing in one ear from being hit by a foul ball . . . but what the world didn't know was that he had diabetes."

"I hadn't heard about that."

"Eventually he had to have both legs amputated. By that time I was attending technical school at night. I'd been tagging along after him for years, helping with the locksmith business in the off-season at first, then later, well, I did all the work." Her hands left her chin and curled into fists on the table.

"I'm sorry, Sarah. I didn't mean to bring up sad memories for you."

"That's all right. They aren't sad. My father never let me be sad, even when we both knew that he was dying. He was special. He started playing with the Crackers when he was only sixteen. He gave up a chance to go to college on a scholarship. Playing baseball was his Pulitzer Prize, his pot of gold. Even when he knew that it was killing him."

"You mean because of the diabetes?"

"Yes. He reached a point when he couldn't tell that he'd been hurt. He had little feeling in his feet and legs."

"But he kept on playing? What did your mother think of that?"

There was a slight pause. "She didn't like it. She never understood that Pop had a different way of seeing everything. Life was to be lived, enjoyed. There was a good side to everything, and he always managed to find it."

"Just like you," Asa said softly, beginning to see where Sarah got her unorthodox approach to life. Her father had found silver linings in the rain clouds and Sarah was doing the same thing. But their rose-colored glasses didn't make the storms go away. And storms could kill you.

"I don't know about that. I do know that we've been given only so much time to live and if we waste it with being negative it only hurts us. Being happy is up to us and we mustn't lose a chance at every bit of what's available."

Sarah uncurled her fingers and lifted her cup. "Drink your coffee before it gets cold."

Asa welcomed the heat of the liquid as he sipped it. "Perfect. You got the sugar right and that rarely happens. People are always trying to change my taste."

"I watched you. Since you're so precise I thought I'd better pay attention."

"Speaking of paying attention, Sarah, I wish you'd be more careful about the message on your answering machine. I know you think there aren't any dishonest people in the world, but there are. Don't invite them to find you by saying there's money under the mat."

"Asa, I'm not as foolish as all that. Even if they looked up my address, they wouldn't bother me. They'd go to the house. And Mother has a burglar alarm that would protect Fort Knox. We're in the locksmith business, remember?"

"Doesn't your mother worry about you?"

"After twenty years with my father she finally decided that it's better to leave me alone. Besides, she's remarried."

"Remarried?"

"She loved my father, but he never understood her. Her new husband is a normal man who lives the kind of normal orderly life she always wanted. Pop would have wanted it for her."

"I hate to say it," Asa observed wryly, "but I can understand her confusion. If her life with your dad was anything like my being with you, she must have felt like she was living in a fantasy half the time."

"Yes. She used to say that being in love with Pop was like being the little girl in an old nursery rhyme she knew. When it was good it was very good . . ."

"But when it was bad, it was horrid."

Sarah gave Asa a long, sad look. "Yes, I guess, for a man like you, the way I live must look pretty horrid."

Asa couldn't keep back a half-smile. "I don't know. At the moment I think I'm too caught up in feeling good."

Sarah looked at Asa's strong face and cloudy gray eyes. He was such a complex man, and there was a vulnerable side to him that drew her. "You know you're taking a risk talking like that."

"I know," he murmured. "It's foolish for me to even be here."

"Yes. I suppose this could be considered very improper. But being here might turn out to be fun. It might even become addictive."

"I know, and it scares the hell out of me."

"Don't feel like that, Asa. Sometimes you have to take risks. There may be pain but we can't appreciate the joy without the sorrow, can we?"

"I don't know. Maybe I've never had any kind of joy to make the comparison."

"Until now, Deputy Canyon. I'm about to show you how to have fun. My kiss is a promise, remember?"

"Forget that," he said ruefully. Anybody that could make me have fun would have to be a genie."

"Maybe I am. Maybe I wrinkled my nose and wished you here."

"Maybe you did. And maybe I'm glad." He stood up and held out his hand.

Sarah moved into his arms and gave herself to his embrace. This time he asked, and he knew that he was asking. When she returned his kiss and pressed herself against him, he accepted and offered himself in return. There was no urgency as they explored each other's mouths, as their hands touched and caressed.

"There's nothing wrong with loving each other," Sarah said, sliding her fingers inside his shirt.

"No, there's nothing wrong with this." His hand was circling her breasts, teasing her nipples through the soft cotton shirt.

"Ahhh!" Sarah couldn't hold back a moan of pleasure.

He stopped kissing her and held her in his arms, rocking her back and forth as he tried to calm his senses.

"Sarah, we have to stop. I can't believe what

I just did, what I'm doing. I should never have come here. This is wrong."

"That's not what you said a minute ago. You said it was good. You're a contradictory man, Deputy Canyon, and I think you're just a little turned on."

Asa dropped his arms and stepped back. She was right. There was no concealing his desire. Nor could he deal with her open statement of fact. He simply couldn't think of an answer of any kind.

"So are you," he finally said.

"Absolutely," she agreed, taking a step forward. "Would you kiss me again?"

"Absolutely not," was his answer. At least he thought it was. "Go to bed," he mumbled, then cursed himself for his inane remark. "I'm leaving now, Sarah. Lock the door behind me, please."

"If you insist."

"Of course I insist. I don't want you to be robbed."

"I mean on leaving."

"I do." He turned and started down the stairs.

"Call me, Asa, when you get home, so I won't worry."

"I can't," he said. "I don't have your number."

"Yes, you do. The shop number rings both places. I'll pick up when you call."

When Asa reached his cabin and dialed her number, he decided to make his words short and sweet.

"Hi, this is Sarah," the recording said. "Please leave a message if you need me and I'll get back to you."

"I'm home, Sarah. Good night. And it was good, very very good," Asa said. As he hung up, he added under his breath, "But I wish it had been horrid."

Five

Sarah drove into the empty parking area adjacent to her building, and looked around. There was no old man waiting for his safe, just as there hadn't been for the past five days.

There was no silver truck either, though she half expected it. Since the night Asa had kissed her in her hayloft, he had either stopped by the barn at night to check on her, or waited at the shop in the mornings. They'd had lunch together a few times in between, talking, getting to know each other, learning that opposites can coexist and draw from each other.

Asa hadn't touched her. They hadn't even held hands. His determination to keep a safe distance between them was driving her crazy. And she was getting very worried about Mr. Grimsley.

Opening the safe had seen so urgent to him,

yet she hadn't heard a word since he'd left the safe. She would have had to report failure, if he'd called. She had tried every conceivable combination and the safe was still locked. Whatever it held was likely to be there for all time, unless she got lucky.

She opened the door and flipped on the air conditioner, breathing a sigh of relief that a cold front was coming through. The state tournament was next week and she didn't look forward to playing in 100 degree August weather. She turned on the answering machine to pick up her calls. There were four inquiries about having dead bolts installed.

The fifth message was a surprise—not the voice, but the request. It was Asa. He must have called just after she left the house, otherwise she'd have heard the phone ringing.

"Sarah, the sheriff's department is sponsoring a booth at the Cotton Patch Days festival on the square Saturday. I've been drafted to help. Would . . . would you like to go? I'd pick you up about eleven o'clock and we'd probably stay through the street dance that follows. I'll call you about seven tonight for your answer."

The rest of the day seemed to fly by. Sarah felt as happy as one of the seven dwarves going off to work. The deputy sheriff had asked her to go out in public with him on a real date. He was making their relationship official. Life couldn't get much better than that.

Jake Dalton called, asking her to take in a

movie on Saturday night. Sarah had to refuse, explaining that she had plans for the weekend.

"Deputy Canyon?"

"Yes."

"I knew it." Jake seemed disappointed but resigned. "Just remember, Sarah, I'm here for you, if it doesn't work."

She could have told Jake that there was nothing to work, not yet. But if she could get Asa to kiss her again, maybe there could be.

Grumpy and Happy. That combination could work. All she needed was a fairy godmother with a wand.

No, that was another story. Still, Pop always told her that a little strategic alteration of the truth could be beneficial. That had been his method of handling her mother when they forgot something they'd been directed to remember under threat of death by hanging or worse.

Besides, Sarah wasn't sure that somebody hadn't already taken a hand. How else could anybody explain her and the deputy, or the kind of fire that ignited when they touched? She'd better hurry. Asa might decide to come by instead of calling.

On the way home, Sarah was stopped at the mailbox by her mother, Alice. "I like your man, Sarah. It's about time you got serious about somebody."

Sarah looked at her mother in shock. For the last two years her mother had been so involved in her new husband that Sarah had seen little of her. "My man?"

"Yes. He stopped by, said he wanted to check the security, something about you leaving money under your mat."

"He *is* worried about me."

"Well, I just thought I'd let you know that he looks like an upright, stable kind of man. Just what a woman needs."

Sarah let those words play through her mind as she drove up the road and pulled in beside the barn. *Stable. Just what a woman needs.* Somehow that smarted. Because she knew that her mother was comparing Asa to her father and her father was coming up short.

She hadn't thought it out, but now she could see that somehow she'd blithely assumed that Asa would loosen up. But maybe she was wrong. There was no question that they were mismatched, just as her parents had been. And Sarah had seen what happened in her parents' marriage.

Sarah wasn't like her mother. She never would be that proper and ladylike. She was like her father, living each day to the fullest without worrying about the next.

But Asa made plans. Asa was orderly and directed. Asa was like her mother.

The invitation to the festival was a perfect example. Having made his decision to invite her to attend, he proceeded to carry it out by calling Sarah, laying out the plan, outlining the schedule and giving her a time when he would call for his answer. The man was totally organized. He'd set a goal and he was halfway to reaching it.

By the time Sarah ran her bath and climbed in for a long soak, she'd come to the conclusion that learning to fly blind into the sun was beyond Asa's ability, and making lists and setting goals were equally foreign to her.

As she dried herself, she kept an ear trained on the phone. When Asa hadn't called by seven-thirty she began to worry. She ate a sandwich and went to work on the safe, trying new combinations of numbers to open it. No luck. By eleven o'clock she still hadn't heard from Asa and she hadn't opened the safe either. She gave up, put out the lights, and went to bed with the latest book by her favorite mystery writer, first making sure the phone was pulled over to the bed.

She watched the minutes tick by, planning what she would say to Asa when he called, and if she should let him know how worried she'd been. She admitted to herself that she was disappointed. She wanted to see him. She wanted to be with him. Why hadn't he called?

Sarah had never chased a man. She hadn't wanted to. Other than her high school sweetheart, there hadn't been a man who interested her. But something told her that if she wanted Asa Canyon she was going to have to do the pursuing. There were ways. She'd just never bothered to learn them.

The only trouble was, she didn't know what the ways were. Sarah knew just one method to go after what she wanted, and that was with honesty and openness. Of course she'd already done that. She'd told him she wanted him. She'd gone to his cabin and kissed him. What else could she do?

Maybe that was the problem. Maybe she was too forward. Men liked being in charge and Asa was more manly than most. Maybe what she needed to do was be subtle. Maybe she needed to talk about this with her mother. Alice was the soul of propriety. Surely she could coach Sarah into being a proper lady who waited until she was asked before throwing herself into a man's arms.

That's what she'd do, first thing in the morning. Sarah snuggled down and turned off the light. She might have to act like a lady tomorrow on her official, proper date with Deputy Canyon, but she could be as wicked as she wanted in her imagination. And right now she could wonder all she liked about what color of underwear Deputy Canyon was wearing.

When she was a little girl she used to say, "I'll close my eyes and count to ten, then I'll get what I want." Sarah closed her eyes and began to count.

It was very late when the phone rang. Sarah dived for it, knocking it in a clatter to the floor.

"Hello, Asa?"

"Yes."

"What's wrong?"

"How do you know something's wrong?"

Sarah could hear the weariness in his voice. "Because you didn't call when you said you would."

"Sorry. I don't usually do that."

"I know. What happened?"

"There was a murder. I've been on the case all night."

"You? I thought the police department handled that."

"Not if it's in the county."

Sarah relaxed, cradling the receiver against her ear and stretching lazily. "You're tired, aren't you? Come over and I'll give you a back rub guaranteed to relax you."

The sleepiness in her voice instantly brought a picture to Asa's mind, a picture of her in bed, a picture of the two of them in bed. There was nothing soothing about that.

"I think not," he said tightly. "If you give me a massage the last thing I'll want to do is relax. Just talking to you is stimulating enough."

"Are you sure? I could make some coffee."

"Sarah, darling, there's something about you and coffee that is, well, let's just say I'm considering taking up drinking tea."

"With lots of cream and sugar."

They were speaking nonsense, but the words didn't matter.

"I like the way you sound when you're waking up," he said. "Your voice is all husky and warm."

"I wish you'd reconsider and come over. You sound so tense and weary."

"I am tense and weary. Murder always does that to me. I have to go now, Sarah. They're waiting for me down in the lab. I just wanted to make sure that you would go to the festival with me today."

"You're still going?"

"The department agreed to have this booth. We have to serve black-eyed peas and cornbread whether an old vagrant is murdered or not."

"Serve peas and cornbread?" Sarah laughed lightly. "I can't see you cooking."

"I'll have you know, I'm a good cook. But today I don't have to make the food, just put it on a plate. I told the Sheriff that you'd give us a hand."

"I'll give you anything you want, Deputy," Sarah said softly.

"Oh, lady—" Asa groaned and dropped the receiver back on its base. She would. He had no doubt of that. And he wanted what she had to give. How long was he going to be able to refuse? How long was he going to tempt himself with the question? How long was he going to be able to keep up a casual relationship with this woman without admitting that he was addicted to her? What kind of fool was he becoming to stand here grinning in the middle of the station?

"Hey, Canyon, did you notice the old guy has no thumb on his right hand?"

"Yeah," he said to the detective who'd just

wandered in. "And he's awful pale, too, like someone who's been sick, or in jail."

The next morning Sarah surprised her mother by joining her at breakfast. Though it was Saturday, Alice's husband, Robert, had gone down to his law office to dictate some letters. Alice was already dressed and drinking her second cup of coffee when Sarah took her old seat at the table.

"Would you like an omelet, Sarah?" Alice asked.

"No, I think what I want is some mother-daughter talk, if you don't mind."

"I'm flattered," Alice admitted, trying to hide the pleasure in her voice.

"It's about Asa."

"I thought it might be."

"He's a lot like you, Mother, and you know how I am. I'm afraid that we don't fit together very well."

Alice filled a cup with coffee and put it down on the table before Sarah. After staring at her for a long time, she said, "That's what my mother said about your father and me."

"Granny?" Sarah could barely remember her grandmother.

"It didn't matter. We were in love. Each of us was sure that the other would change."

"But you didn't, did you?"

"No, we tried, but we didn't. People have to be what they are, I think, or they're very unhappy."

Sarah left her chair and walked over to the window. "That's what I thought." She opened the door and started to go out.

"No, Sarah, you don't understand. Being different didn't make us love each other less. It just made the loving more intense. I might have changed our lives if I could have, but I would never have chosen a different man."

Sarah drove down to the shop half expecting to find Mr. Grimsley. She didn't. She was beginning to think that she wasn't going to hear from him again. It wouldn't be the first time somebody brought something in and never came back for it. But she had the impression that Mr. Grimsley was very anxious about his safe. She was beginning to be a little anxious herself. Dynamite might be the only answer.

After waiting an hour, working on various projects, Sarah gave up. She left a note taped to the window and went home. It was Saturday and she had a festival to go to.

No luck on the safe, Mr. G. Still working on it. Call me.

By eleven o'clock she had dressed and undressed three times. The dress she'd started with made her look very proper, but she'd never be able to serve black-eyed peas wearing that. Next she'd pulled on cutoffs and a T-shirt, which she discarded as being too informal. Now she was wearing a short, full-cut red cotton knit skirt with a matching red top that left her midriff bare. A pair of red canvas tennis shoes and white socks completed her outfit.

She wouldn't have any trouble getting into Asa's truck dressed like this.

When she heard the horn blowing she ran to the hayloft doors and pushed one side open. Asa was standing beside the truck looking up at her. Sarah felt her heart slam against her rib cage.

"Ready?"

Ready? One look at him and she knew that was the right word. His gray eyes seemed lighter this morning, more in tune with the clean-shaven face and the neatly combed dark hair. He was wearing jeans, formfitting ones that covered the tops of western pointed-toe boots. His plaid shirt was red and he wore a bandana tied at the neck.

Oh yes, she was ready. She was so ready that she was tempted to catch the rope pulley and swing out of the loft.

"Want to come up?" she asked brightly.

He actually grinned, running his fingers through his hair, mussing it as if he was embarrassed to be seen smiling. "I think that would be a mistake."

She disagreed, but now wasn't the time to argue. Instead, she closed the door and cast a guilty look at the safe. Tomorrow she'd spend all day on it until she got it open.

When she stepped into the sunlight Asa

swallowed his grin, along with his breath. The short skirt she was wearing flared out like a tennis dress and he wondered how he would get through the morning. "What do you call that, whatever it is you're wearing?" he asked.

"It's just called mix and match separates. Nothing special," she answered, beginning to understand that the day was going to be another test in different life-styles. "Why? Don't you like it?"

"I'm not sure. It's certainly different."

"If you'd rather, I'll go back and put on a dress." Sarah slid across the truck seat and leaned toward him. She would change her clothes if he insisted, but she'd make him sorry he asked.

"Eh . . . no. Whatever makes you comfortable," he managed to say.

Sarah gave Asa a quick kiss before she moved back to her side of the truck. "Where's your badge, Deputy?"

"Today I'm off duty," he replied.

"Somehow I can't see you serving black-eyed peas in a park, Deputy Canyon."

"Oh? I'll have you know that once I worked as a short-order cook in a club called the Lucky Nugget in Vegas."

Sarah gave him her best "I don't believe you" look. "What were you doing there? You don't look like a gambler."

"I'm not. I only take chances on myself."

Sarah could believe that. Taking a chance was releasing control and she already knew

that Deputy Asa Canyon was always in control
of his own fate. "What did you cook?"

"Chili and beans, steaks, burgers."

"Somehow I can't visualize you behind a
stove."

"It didn't last long."

"What happened?"

"The manager fired me. He didn't like my
recipes."

"What was wrong with them?"

"I used real meat in the burgers, and prime
steaks on the grill. People started to eat instead of drink and gamble. Food wasn't as
profitable."

"And cheaper cuts and more beans would
never be acceptable for you, would they?"

"You got it, Sarah. If a man is going to do a
thing, he ought to do it well. By the way, I
picked up some spare lumber yesterday. I'll
make you another shelf or two in your pantry
so that you can organize your food better."

"Asa, I hate to tell you, but I don't have that
much to organize. I'm more into fast food.
Since I don't cook I don't need to know where
anything is, do I?"

Asa started to reply, then caught sight of
her expression and concentrated on his driving. She couldn't see the value in keeping her
pantry in order, but he'd teach her. There
were so many things he could share with her
when she relaxed and stopped trying to be
such a rebel.

When? What was he thinking? This woman
would never be any more practical than she

was now. She didn't know how and wouldn't want to be if she did. He didn't know why he was even thinking along those lines. He didn't even know why he was still here.

The Cobb sheriff's department wasn't where he belonged, at least not forever. He'd only taken the job because Jeanie had needed him. Now she was gone. Sooner or later he'd have to get back on track.

Sarah didn't need him. Sarah wasn't his responsibility. Sarah was a breath of fresh air, and bottled air lost its potency. He never wanted her to lose that special zest for life that she carried around like an aura.

This morning she was wearing a different perfume. It was crisp, lightly sweet, like the fragrance of a meadow of wildflowers. He could almost picture her in the springtime, in the mountains. She'd be standing by a running stream, surrounded by rhododendrons, waiting for . . . him.

By the time they parked in Asa's reserved space at the sheriff's department just off the courthouse square, Asa was wondering what he had started by inviting Sarah to come along. She couldn't help but see this as a date. She couldn't mistake his interest either.

Sarah hadn't commented on being called for duty at the Sheriff's booth. She wasn't quite sure what Asa expected from the day. She finally decided that trying to formulate a plan that would please Asa was foolish. Even if she made one, she was unlikely to follow it.

By now Asa surely knew what kind of person she was. She couldn't be something she wasn't, and neither could he. Today would be a good test of whether or not their relationship could survive the outside world.

She gave a quick little sigh. Their relationship. Dare she even go that far? Yes, she decided, she could. And this was the start. Where they went from here, she couldn't control and neither could Asa. They would just have to follow the winds of chance. Because, whether or not Asa wanted to admit it, they'd stirred up a whirlwind and every time they were together the intensity grew.

By two o'clock everybody in Cobb County had brought their plate for a ladle of the Sheriff's special black-eyed peas. Sarah had added a chunk of hot cornbread and a greeting. More than one of the local ladies had come through for a second helping and an invitation for Asa Canyon to join them. He thanked each of them, then said he'd check with Sarah about attending. Once Sarah's name got officially linked to Asa's, Asa's line shortened. Sarah's friends kept on with the wisecracks and warm hellos.

"Do you really know everybody in the county, Sarah?"

"No, there are always a few newcomers. But sooner or later, I get to know most of them."

Perspiration was running down Asa's face. His eyes felt like they were filled with dry sand. For all practical purposes he hadn't slept since he'd met Sarah Wilson. He didn't know why he was standing out here in the sun serving peas when he ought to be finding the murderer of the vagrant they'd found last night in the county park.

The autopsy was underway now. Ballistics experts were checking the bullets that had been fired into the body before it was thrown in the lake. Fingerprints were being run through the FBI headquarters in Washington and the victim's clothes were being examined in the lab. Until the reports were in, Asa had been instructed to man the pot of peas at the festival.

He finally figured out that part of his reservations was because he wasn't doing his job, and part of them was because he was tired of sharing Sarah with the world.

"What's wrong, Deputy? Are you hot?" Sarah had moved closer to Asa, concern marring her sunny expression.

His gaze followed a bead of perspiration trickling down her neck, rolling past her collarbone, disappearing into the body-hugging stretch top she was wearing.

"Yes, I'm very warm," he said.

"Then I think it's time we had a break. Hey, guys," she called to the officers kibitzing behind them. "Time for a shift change."

Sarah picked up two cups of lemonade and managed to avoid drawn out conversations with festival-goers as she and Asa sipped the cool drinks and made their way through the crowd.

The city square was filled with people: Craftsmen with their wares and locals who enjoyed the food and activities. Asa couldn't imagine where the two of them were heading until Sarah dropped their cups in a trash can, took his hand, and led him across the street.

"Where are we going?"

"Don't ask questions. Just follow me."

He did.

They ducked into an alley behind the row of buildings on the north side of the square. When they reached the last building Sarah fumbled with a panel beside a small side entrance. When the door swung open she jerked Asa inside and closed it behind them. The room was cool and totally dark.

"Where exactly are we?" he asked.

"We're on the stage of the old Strand Theater, behind the curtain."

"A movie theater?"

"Well, it isn't a movie house anymore. It's being used as a theater."

Asa whistled. She'd done it again, caught him off guard. "How'd we get in? Wasn't it locked?"

"Yes, but I put the lock in and I know the combination. The owner left my code in the alarm, in case I ever had to make a service call."

"Then we're not trespassing?"

"Oh, I didn't say that. Come on." She took his hand and pulled him forward. Trying to see was impossible and after slamming into two pieces of equipment, Sarah finally pulled his arms around her so that they were curled together like two spoons as they walked.

"Now stay with me," she said.

"Are you sure we're alone here?" Asa asked, concerned about the growing evidence of his reaction to her nearness.

"Why, Deputy, you want to fool around?"

Sarah twisted around in his arms and pulled his face down to meet hers. "Do I embarrass you, Asa?"

"No! Yes! Hell, I don't know what you do to me. I just know that I've broken into a building and I'm standing here in the dark making out with a woman who doesn't have any idea what she's inviting!"

"I think I know," she said in a voice that was throaty with desire. "I'm inviting you to kiss me."

"As I recall, you were taking me someplace to get cooled off."

"Not true. I asked you if you were hot and you agreed. I figured that I'd never get a better shot at taking advantage of you."

He groaned. She was right. He wanted badly to kiss her. Just one quick intense little kiss wasn't going to make things any worse than they already were.

"Asa?"

"I like the way you say my name, Sarah. I like the way you smell, the way you feel." He pressed a hand against the small of her back. He planted the other on her bare skin just below the swell of her breasts.

"Asa," she whispered, and rose up on her toes.

Then he covered her mouth with his in a hard, possessive kiss, parting her lips, plunging his tongue deep inside as he pulled her even closer. She copied his movements, shifting her body so that every part of them could touch. He was murmuring her name now as his fingers slid beneath her top and claimed her breasts.

She could have cried out with joy if he hadn't been stealing her breath with his mouth. There was something warm and wonderful exploding inside her, something that she would have stopped to consider except she was too busy feeling pleasure.

Asa was lost. From the moment he took her into his arms he was overwhelmed with emotion. Her scent filled his nostrils. Her body filled his hands. The joy of being with her erased all sense of caution and he gave into his desire. As he bent over her, sliding his mouth down her neck and across her breasts his arms came in contact with something metallic. It moved and they fell forward, just as the curtains slid open and the stage lights came on, flooding them with brightness.

Asa stood up, lifting Sarah. "Damn! I can't see a thing. It's too bright."

"Oh, Asa," Sarah was whispering. "I never knew kissing could be so . . . illuminating."

"Damn!" Asa swore again. "What kind of cooling-off place is this?" He was beginning to adjust to the lights. At the other end of the building, where he'd expected to see a partition between the seats and the lobby, was a plate glass window. They were in full view of the entire square.

"Cooling off?" Sarah's innocent quip was lost on Asa as he observed the applause of the onlookers on the sidewalk.

"Damn! Let's get out of here!" Asa whirled around and threw the light switch. "I hope you know how to relock this door."

"It locks automatically."

"Fine." There was no more conversation as he dragged Sarah behind the buildings to his truck. He helped her in, climbed in beside her, and slammed the door.

"What is there about you and lights?" he asked, knowing that he was bellowing and knowing that he couldn't stop himself. "Don't you ever stop to think what your actions can lead to?"

"I thought it was nice. I like kissing you. I like touching you. I like you touching me. But I can understand I embarrass you. You aren't very public with your feelings. I keep forgetting and I'm sorry about that, but I won't apologize for the way I feel."

Asa took a deep breath.

"It isn't you, Sarah. It's me. I've been alone so long that I don't know how to act with a woman."

"I think you do very well."

"I think I'd better take you home."

"Aren't we going to stay for the dance?"

Dance? Hold Sarah in his arms with the

world watching? Not today! Not tomorrow! Not ever! Asa gripped the steering wheel tightly, trying desperately to formulate an answer. He failed. Instead, he found himself turning toward Sarah, leaning forward, taking her into his arms. What he might have done he'd never know for at that moment the shortwave radio in his truck crackled on.

"Are you there, Deputy? We have a problem."

Asa pulled away and picked up the speaker. "Canyon here. What do you have?"

"We've got a make on our body. You'd better come in."

"Damn!" This time it was Sarah who cursed and drew back in frustration.

Six

Asa kept the engine running when he pulled up to the fence outside her barn. Sarah knew that he was impatient to get to his office but she couldn't resist asking, "Will you come by later?"

"I don't know. I have a job to do. I can't—" He stopped, softened his voice and added, "If I don't come, I'll try to call you."

That was more than she'd expected. Sarah slid out, started to the barn, stopped and turned back.

"I'll be here, Asa. People aren't always temporary."

Her words played through his mind as he drove back to the station. *People aren't always temporary.* He wanted to believe her, but he didn't dare.

Sarah Wilson was the kindest, most caring person in the world, but other caring people had abandoned him, and she would be no exception.

Jeanie had left. This was the first time he'd allowed himself to admit that Jeanie's running away with Mike hurt. In spite of all his resolve, Jeanie had become family. And for her to elope without talking it over with him was a blow.

Now there was Sarah. He didn't know why he'd let things with Sarah go so far. Except that he cared for her. She made him feel wanted in a way that wasn't just sexual. And no matter how hard he tried not to, he admitted that he wanted to be wanted.

Still, Sarah was temporary. Sooner or later she'd grow tired of him and she'd move on to the next poor lost soul. Rescuing people seemed to be her thing. As long as he kept reminding himself of that it wouldn't hurt when she left. He wouldn't let it. He wouldn't feel it.

Yes, you will, a little voice whispered. *But maybe this time, the caring is worth the pain.*

After Asa left, Sarah tried some more combinations on the safe, all without success. Then she recalled that her father had had several antique books on locks. She decided to make a couple of service calls while Asa was working and afterward do some research on the safe. That way she'd be here if Asa called. Recording a message on her answering machine that told her current plans, she changed clothes and started on her rounds.

It was late afternoon when she finished the last call and stopped by the shop to pick up a new pair of handcuffs and keys. She intended to offer them to Asa as replacement for the ones she'd destroyed. On the way home she dropped by the market for steaks and salad greens, which would be, she hoped, her first meal for Deputy Canyon. As she turned down the drive she stopped and ran inside the house where her mother was peeling apples from the trees Sarah and Big Jim had planted.

"Sarah, come in. How nice to see you. Aren't the apples nice?"

"Yes."

There was a long silence before Sarah's mother asked, "Is there something wrong, Sarah?"

"No. Yes. Maybe. I came to borrow some of Pop's antique reference books. But if you have time, I think I'd like to talk about . . . about . . ."

"He's something to talk about all right," her mother said.

"He?" Sarah started to protest, looked at her mother and changed her mind. "Yes, I think he is."

"He seems to be a very private man. But when he came by to check my security system, I asked him what his intentions were toward you, and he confessed. Besides, I think he really wanted to talk."

"You asked him what his intentions were?" Sarah groaned. "Mother, I don't believe you."

"Well, your father isn't here. I felt it was my duty."

"What makes you think Asa wanted to talk?"

"He seemed so concerned about security. He really checked out the house. When he got to your old room, he must have asked a hundred questions."

"Like what?"

"Like why you moved into the barn, and why you weren't married."

"Oh. What did you tell him?"

"The truth. That you moved out there because you and your father had so many happy times there, and that you never married because you were afraid to let yourself care for somebody else who might leave you. I think he understood that answer."

"But that's not true. I left the house so that you and Robert would be more comfortable. No man wants to come into a marriage with an adult daughter living in the house. As for Pop, he told me over and over that I should find myself somebody to love. I just . . . haven't."

"That's because you never let anybody get beyond the friendship stage, do you? Look at Paul Martin and Jake Dalton. Both men care for you but you never seem to notice. Why this one?"

"I don't know," Sarah answered her mother

honestly. "He just seems to be in so much pain."

"Like your father? Oh, Sarah, if you love a man, love him for the right reasons, not because he's in need of comfort."

"I know. That's why I'm so confused. Mother, were you . . . were you happy with Pop?"

"Not always. But"—she stared out into space—"I was never unhappy. Confused is a word that might fit my feelings too. He was larger than life, and I could never claim him all for myself. A part of him was mine, but the rest belonged to everyone who needed something from him."

"But didn't that make you crazy?"

"For a while, but I came to understand that I was very lucky that there was a part for me. You're just like your father, Sarah. And I always worried that you wouldn't find a man who would share you. I'm not worried anymore. Asa is strong enough. He doesn't know how to love yet, so you'll just have to teach him."

"Did Pop teach you?"

"We taught each other."

"But I always thought that you disapproved of him."

"I was angry that he was going to die when I thought he might have been able to live longer if he'd been more careful. I didn't want him to go on playing baseball. The doctors said it was too much of a strain on his body. I threatened to leave him if he didn't quit."

Sarah gave a quiet gasp. Her mother leave her father? She'd known that their marriage hadn't always been happy, but she couldn't imagine either of them not being married to each other.

"I begged him to get a regular job," her mother went on, "like my friends' husbands. I thought if things were normal, he'd be normal. He tried it for one winter, and it almost killed him. Oh, he was stronger physically, but he was not the same man.

"Finally I understood what I was doing to him. My fear was making us both unhappy so I sent him off to spring training the next year. I never tried to change him again."

Alice took a deep breath and picked up another apple. "I'm making apples pies, darling. Would you like one for Deputy Canyon?"

Sarah felt dazed. Her mother rarely talked about personal thoughts. She always kept everything to herself. Yet in the last five minutes she'd divulged more about her pain and regrets than she'd ever done before. She'd done it to make Sarah see that differences didn't always destroy, not if two people loved each other.

"I'd love a pie," Sarah finally said, "as long as it has a 'Made by Alice' label on it."

"Made by Alice? What does that mean?"

"It means I don't want Asa to get the idea that I can cook. He knows about my coffee. This pie would blow my image."

"Oh, he won't think that. I already told him you can't cook. I told him that you get the hiccups when you're excited and that you're silly about Christmas, too."

"You didn't."

"And you know what I learned? The man has never put up a Christmas tree. I told him not to worry. You always cut your own and put it up the day after Thanksgiving. So you'd better start looking for one that's huge. I think Deputy Canyon needs a tree big enough to make up for all the ones he's missed."

The potatoes were in the microwave ready for baking. The steaks were in the oven broiler. The salad was in the refrigerator. Sarah stirred sugar into the pitcher of tea she'd just made and sat down to read about old safes in the reference books and watch the news while she waited.

Channel Eight had a brief story on the drowning of an unidentified elderly man whose body had been found floating in the river by the park the night before. They were not releasing his name until next of kin had been notified. Foul play was suspected. It was believed that the man had been one of the vagrants who lived under an overpass nearby.

Sarah was about to change the channel when the camera caught Asa in its pan across the activity along the river bank. He was grim-faced and impatient, pushing past the reporter without acknowledging the television personality's attempt to question him.

"That was Deputy Sheriff Asa Canyon," the

reporter said. "He's the same deputy who apprehended the two men who robbed a drive-in restaurant three weeks ago. Deputy Canyon, an ex-Marine, came to Cobb County from Stevens Securities, where he served as project director for the last five years."

A Marine was always the first on the scene of any confrontation, Sarah mused. He was loyal, dependable, and took care of business. Something like a boy scout, she thought, smiling. She remembered what her mother had said about Christmas trees and wondered if Asa liked gingerbread men.

A drop of perspiration ran down her forehead. Sarah turned the air conditioning up a notch. Gingerbread men. Christmas trees. It was August and the mercury in the thermometer outside the window was still clinging to 90 degrees. Well, she could dream about fall. She could close her eyes and count to ten, too, if she thought it would make her phone ring.

"It didn't.

"He wasn't just a vagrant," the sheriff said. "Name was Lincoln Grimsley. Seems like our boy just got himself released from a federal pen. Been spending the last fifteen years there, off and on."

Asa looked at the report and scowled. "What for?"

"Larceny. At one time or another, he's tried most everything. According to his rap sheet, he married six women and took all their life savings, swindled at least four others of various amounts of money, and turned to mail fraud. Mostly he was just a lousy con man. Kept getting caught. Seems he was a talker. Couldn't keep his mouth shut."

"So what's he doing here?"

"That's the surprise. He was a distant relative of the Grimsley family."

The sheriff struck a big wooden kitchen match and lit the filter-tipped cigarette in his mouth. Then he opened a manila envelope and spread the contents across the desk top.

Asa picked up the leather change purse held together with cords of matching rawhide. The purse, waterlogged and still damp, held three dollar bills and a handful of change.

Using the matchstick, the sheriff shoved a scrap of newspaper toward Asa. He read the clipping, which was about the new Smyrna Village and the refurbishing of the old Grimsley House and the adjacent one-hundred-and-thirty-year-old Bank of Smyrna building.

"He knew about the project. Then as soon as he got out of prison he came straight here. Why?" the sheriff asked.

"Now there's the two-dollar question. I'm going to run over to Smyrna City Hall and ask a few questions."

"Go ahead, but remember, the less anybody knows about this, the better. We don't want everyone horning in. Too many cooks spoil the soup, or whatever that old saying is."

"Right, Chief." Asa gave his boss a nod and left the office.

He glanced at his watch as he got into his truck. He'd told Sarah he'd call her. He didn't know why he'd done that. It put a routine in their relationship, and he hadn't intended to establish one. Taking her to the Cotton Patch Days Festival was a mistake, too. He'd known it at the time. If he hadn't, seeing her in that short skirt and brief top should have made it very clear.

Having her come with him had been arranged without Asa's knowing. Something had been said about his playing on Sarah's softball team. The sheriff had complimented Asa on his zeroing in on the nicest girl in the county. And suddenly Asa was agreeing to ask Sarah to help out in the booth.

The sheriff was right about one thing. Sarah Wilson was special. He'd never known anyone like her. She was the all-American girl, a natural athlete and fervent do-gooder. She cut down her own Christmas tree and put it up the day after Thanksgiving. She was spotted puppies and picket fences and every time he was around her he could almost feel the pointed fence posts digging into his back.

Sarah was a distraction.

Sarah was a mistake.

But Sarah was all he'd thought about for the last few days. She didn't make him feel like a jaded thirty-five, more like an exuberant seventeen.

There was a phone booth beside the service

station at the corner, and although he knew better, he pulled in.

The phone rang only once before she answered. "Deputy?"

"Of course. Who did you expect?"

"You. I'm just waiting to find out which one of you it is, Dirty Harry or Asa."

Asa could imagine her sitting cross-legged in bed, leaning back against her pillow, her hair mussed, her arm folded behind her head as she cradled the phone against her ear.

"Which do you want?"

"Well, I'll take either one, but I'd like to have a little talk with the guy who's worried about my security system."

"Oh, you know about that."

"I also know that Mother thinks you're perfect for me, once I teach you about loving somebody."

Asa tried to answer, but his voice stuck in his throat and he couldn't utter a word. He just stood there, hearing his heart beat like thunder in his ear.

"Are you still there, Asa?"

He cleared his throat. "I think we'd better talk, Sarah," he finally managed to say.

"When?"

"Later."

"I'll have supper for you."

"You can't cook. Your mother told me."

"Even I can manage steak and potatoes."

"I can't stay."

"You don't have to."

Asa rubbed his eyes. He was tired. Too tired,

and he had to eat somewhere. What she was saying was too appealing. He heard himself agreeing.

"All right. I'll be there, when I can."

"I'll be waiting."

City Hall was closed on Saturday afternoon, but the police station next door was doing a brisk business. The officer on duty directed him through a maze of offices to the captain.

"Asa Canyon, Captain." Asa held out his hand and felt the rough grip of the prematurely gray-haired officer behind the desk.

"Snow Sims, here. Heard about you, Canyon. Pull up a chair. What can the Smyrna Police Department do for you?"

He told the captain about Lincoln Grimsley and why he needed to take a look at the Grimsley house.

"You'll have to wait," Snow Sims said. "The old key disappeared and somebody was seen in the house. The historical society folks put a new lock on it. Now only the supervisor has a key, and he won't be back till Monday."

Asa glanced at his watch. Almost seven. He exchanged the expected pleasantries with the captain and left, driving by the Smyrna Village construction site. Asa hadn't realized that the bank was still in use until he saw a temporary entrance at the back of the building.

On the way to Sarah's place, he puzzled over the connection between the old man's death and the house. Why would he have come here after all these years? And was his death related to the house?

By the time he reached Sarah's red barn he was still as confused as he had been when he'd left the police station. He didn't even knock. He knew the door would be open.

His boots made a thudding sound as he walked along the side of the basketball court and up the stairs. When he was halfway up, the door flung open and Sarah's voice called out.

"Hurry, please."

He covered the last three risers with one long step and walked into Sarah's welcoming embrace. He'd waited all day for her kiss. Hell, he'd waited all his life for it. Foolish or not, he couldn't turn it down.

His arms slid around her, his hands tightening into fists as he tried to hold back. But he knew that tonight, there was no turning back. His mouth closed over hers, slowly, gently. She tasted sweet, as if she'd been eating brown sugar and cinnamon. There was a tantalizing smell of spice in the air.

Sarah sighed, lifting her hands to the back of his neck and spreading her fingers through his hair. Her very touch was intoxicating and he knew that she was as drunk with desire as he. He'd never been so aware of a woman's touch, of the scent and taste that separated Sarah from all others. She stirred his senses, making him feel more alive.

Sarah's thoughts were less coherent, less rational. She only knew that Asa was here and that was all she wanted. Her sigh turned into a low moan as the warmth of his touch brought her body to a fevered pitch. Her breasts began to burn. Colors swirled behind her eyelids, like a kaleidoscope of shades and lights that merged, separated, and reshaped themselves as the kiss went on.

Then she heard a groan of anguish as Asa's hands suddenly came to life and captured her bottom, pulling her savagely against him. And she knew that this man was as helpless against his need as she was against her own.

She pulled back. Tearing her lips from his she drew in a long breath. Asa leaned his forehead against her head and swallowed hard. Sarah didn't know what he was about to say, but she was certain that he had already started marshaling his forces to withdraw. She couldn't let that happen, not again.

"No," she whispered, kissing him lightly. "Don't talk. Don't explain or excuse. Just be with me."

She slipped her fingers inside his shirt and began to unbutton it, skimming the matted curls of his chest hair beneath her touch. She felt him catch his breath when she tugged his shirt from his jeans and unbuckled his belt.

"Do you know what you're doing, lady?"

"No. But I'm a fast learner."

The zipper slid open smoothly and she shoved his jeans down his legs. Catching sight of his underwear she began to grin. "Black? You're a wicked man, Asa Canyon."

"I'm a—" He started to say, aroused man,

but he realized that wasn't necessary. His condition boldly announced itself.

Asa stepped back, balancing himself as he tugged his boots off one at a time and stepped out of his jeans. When he raised his eyes again he gasped.

Sarah was standing before him, completely nude, her proud breasts trembling with every uneven breath she took.

"Are you sure, Sarah?"

"I've never been more sure of anything."

He could see the fear in her eyes, but she was standing there, admitting her desire and asking him to make love to her. Suddenly he realized that this was what it was like to feel love, to want a woman so much that you're afraid to touch her, to know that she's giving herself to you with no regrets and no conditions, to feel certain that she's the missing part of yourself.

Sarah knew that she was swaying, that her breasts hurt with longing and that her insides were churning wildly under his gaze. She'd never been so bold before. She'd never wanted to. Now she could do nothing but offer herself and wait.

"Sarah." His voice was gravelly, as though he could barely speak. "Sarah, I want to make love to you. I want to touch you, fill you with my body and lose myself in your heat."

"I want you, too, Asa. But I'm scared. It's been so long since I've been . . . with a man. I'm not very experienced. I'm afraid that I'll disappoint a man like you."

Sarah knew that if he didn't take her in his arms again she was going to fall apart and dissolve into thin air. She couldn't be so close and not touch him. With a half-gasp she leaned forward, letting her nipples skim his chest, feeling the hair brush against her like tiny electric fingers.

"Please, Asa."

"Sarah, listen to me. This isn't easy and it may be the last rational statement I'll ever make to you. Whatever I may feel for you, I can't make any promises. I don't expect any from you. No commitment. No tomorrow. Can you accept that?"

She raised her flushed face and gazed into his eyes. Her lips were parted and he could feel tiny puffs of air as she breathed in and out.

"I don't know," she said softly. "I just know that we should do what we have to." She reached up and pulled his face down to hers, kissing him, holding him with a tenderness that was stronger than bands of steel, drinking his essence as if she knew that she'd never be with him again.

Asa lifted her in his arms and walked down the tiny corridor into her room. Sarah's bed was a mattress on a built-up platform and covered with pillows.

He knelt down, lowered her until her back was against the pillows, his knee between her legs. He could feel her body hair feathering his kneecap as he began to kiss her, skimming her face with his mouth, tasting, memorizing her features.

A smile stretching across her face, Sarah openly watched him. No pulling back, no restraint. A coil of heat began to writhe in her lower body as she ran her fingers up and down Asa's back, across his chest, circling his nipples and tracing the cords of muscle in his arms.

He pressed himself against her, or maybe she reached out to touch him. She didn't know. She only knew that they were still too much apart. She lifted her arms to pull him closer.

She was no longer the inexperienced child of seventeen she had been the first time. Now she was a woman and no matter what had happened before, this was new. She'd never suspected that loving could be so good. There was no awkwardness, no embarrassment, only a feeling of rightness, as if they'd been drawn together in some sort of natural plan that was unfolding around them like a rare night-blooming flower.

And then they were together, completely, joined as lovers, moving through the intricate dance of the senses. They were touching as if they'd never touched before and never would again, as if already they knew that they would lose their capacity to feel in the light of day and this night was all there would ever be.

Asa had never known such intense pleasure, nor had he ever wanted so much to give joy to a woman as he wanted to now. When he breathed he shared the same air that she breathed. When he moved she followed his motion. They were like two leaves joined in a stream, rushing headlong into the white waters that flung them over the edge.

Afterward they were drifting, holding each other, both stunned by the wonder of what they'd just experienced. Slippery bodies began to dry. Desire turned into fulfillment and the unknown became one priceless moment of belonging.

Sarah lay with her head on Asa's chest, one leg flung across his lower body. She held on to him, unwilling to move for fear of separating from this man who had suddenly become the center of her being.

After a time, she recognized the old tension gathering in his body, and she stretched, sliding her leg even higher, wanting to gather him to her so that their parting wouldn't come.

"Hey, I thought it was the woman who was supposed to have regrets," she said.

"And do you?" His voice was tense.

"Not one. If I never have your love, I'll have had this."

"And that's enough?"

"No, but I'll try not to be too greedy. I'm not one of those temporary people in your life, Asa, but I'll never be a weight around your neck either."

"Sarah, listen to me. All my life people have pulled away from me. Oh, they'd start off by making me think that they wanted me, but sooner or later, they left. You will too. I know."

"Not me. Truth is, if you want me, big boy,"

she said with exaggerated huskiness, "all you have to do is whistle."

"Don't make jokes." Asa pulled her over him, his forehead creased into a deep frown. "I don't want to feel this way, as if we're connected somehow and belong together. But I do, and I'm scared."

Sarah looked deeply into Asa's eyes. She could see the little boy who was rejected, who was returned over and over again to the orphanage, and she could feel the hurt he'd known. Now, he was trying to build a wall between them by rejecting her. But even as she stared down at him, she felt the wall begin to collapse.

"Don't be," she whispered and kissed him. As their bodies found new ways to fit together, their lips spoke words of promise that banished all their fears. The first time they came together Asa loved Sarah. This time Sarah loved him back.

Later they lay entwined, sated, happy. The sky was black. Through the window the stars gleamed in the night sky.

"Are you ready to eat?" Sarah finally asked.

"I don't think I can walk to the kitchen," Asa admitted.

"Then I'll bring the food to you."

He came to one elbow and looked at her. "You already have."

"That was food for the soul, Asa. Now I intend to nourish your body." She grinned and slipped unselfconsciously from the bed.

Sarah was tying the sash of her robe when

the phone rang. Captain Sims from the Smyrna Police Department was looking for Asa. She handed him the phone, covering the receiver as she whispered, "Snow Sims, for you."

Asa sat up, wondering how the captain knew he was with Sarah. "Yes."

"Sorry to bother you, but I just talked to Paul Martin."

Aha! Officer Martin must have told Sims to call Sarah's number.

"You'd better get over to Sarah's shop," Sims went on.

"Why?"

"You're not going to believe this, but somebody's trashed it big time."

A chill ran over Asa. When he was a child one of his foster mothers had been fond of the phrase, "A rabbit just ran over my grave."

Asa knew now what the phrase meant.

Seven

"Why would anybody do this?"

Sarah stood in the middle of her shop, turning slowly around. The place hadn't just been ransacked, it had been destroyed. The windows were broken. The shelves had been split. All the equipment was upturned and her stock had been unboxed and piled in the middle of the floor.

Frowning, Asa studied the destruction. He felt great rage that someone had violated Sarah's shop. This was her place, a part of her. Whoever did this couldn't have known Sarah or it would never have happened.

"Why?" she repeated.

Asa reached out, put his arms around Sarah, and held her.

"I don't know why, Sarah. Vandals. Some kids having fun. I don't know. Did you keep any money here?"

She laughed. "Me? No, I don't get much cash. There were a few checks. They were in a box under the counter."

Sarah pulled away and walked over to what used to be her counter. The box was still underneath, along with her receipt book and the container that had held her claim tickets.

Officer Paul Martin was directing other officers in searching the building for evidence. "Glad you're here, Asa. They broke in through the back door. Wasn't even a professional job. Somebody just picked up a rock, broke the glass, and reached inside to open the door."

Asa turned to Sarah.

"I thought you were in the security business. Don't you have some kind of burglar alarm here?"

"Good heavens, no. I've even been known to leave the door unlocked. If they'd tried they probably could have walked right in. Why would anybody break in? Everybody knows I don't keep cash here."

"There must have been something here, something that somebody was looking for," Asa insisted. "Think, Sarah."

"No. I don't have anything valuable, not unless—wait a minute. The old man."

"What old man?"

"He came in last week just before I closed. He had an old safe that he wanted me to open."

"Lincoln Grimsley," Paul said.

"Grimsley was here?" Asa turned a disbelieving look toward Sarah.

"Yes. Do you know him?" Sarah asked, as Asa took her arm and pulled her over to one corner, away from the officers who were taking fingerprints on the counter.

Paul followed. "Lincoln Grimsley was an ex-con, just got out of jail. Checked in over at the department last week when he first got to town. Just wanted to see his old family home. Seemed harmless enough."

"That's why he was so pale," Sarah muttered. "I thought he'd been sick."

"Tell us about the safe, Sarah," Asa told her, trying to remain calm despite the fear growing in him.

"Well, he was very anxious about opening it. It was pretty small and he didn't want it destroyed. He was supposed to come back Monday morning. He never showed up."

"I think we know why," Asa declared.

Paul caught Asa's worried expression. "Did you notice anything else unusual about him, Sarah?"

"He was polite. He seemed nervous. Oh, and he was missing a thumb on his right hand."

"That was definitely him," Paul stated.

Asa paced back and forth, a frown on his face. "What about the safe? Any idea where he got it?"

"Don't know anything about that," Paul answered. "He didn't have it when I saw him. But he did call back later asking about locksmiths." He groaned. "I recommended Sarah."

"I'd say," Captain Sims commented, "that he found the safe in the house."

They were talking back and forth as if Sarah wasn't there. "He did," she interjected. "There was a family legend that said it was there, that it contained the family treasure. He said that the renovators had found an old room that had been sealed off. The safe was inside."

Captain Sims nodded. "Treasure. Now we're getting somewhere."

"No," Sarah said. "The safe was too light to have gold or silver, so Mr. Grimsley figured it was filled with Confederate paper money."

"Is it?" Asa and Paul inquired at once.

"I don't know. The numbers are worn off on the lock and I can't figure out the combination."

"Then whoever killed him must be after the safe." Asa let out a sigh.

"Men, keep a watch out for a small safe. It would be something that could be carried about, wouldn't it?" Paul asked, turning to Sarah for a description.

She shook her head. "Oh, it isn't here. I took it home with me."

"You have it? That explains everything," Paul said happily. "That's why everything is torn apart. They didn't find it. Maybe they don't know for sure that you have it. Maybe they're still looking."

"I agree," Asa said, the grooves in his forehead deepening.

"In that case"—Sims took a last look around—"I think we've done about all we can do tonight. You men close the place as best you can and we'll look around some more in the daylight."

Asa watched the burglary team file out and drive away. He turned to Sims. "We'd better put out a notice to the other locksmiths in the area."

"Done."

"At least they didn't come to the shop while you were here, Sarah," Asa said quietly.

"I think we can assume that they won't be back here. Sarah ought to be safe," Paul declared.

"But I'm afraid they may know that I still have it," Sarah put in. "I just remembered. I left Mr. Grimsley a note on the door, saying I hadn't been able to open the safe and to call me."

"Damn!" Asa's voice dropped an octave. "Is it still there?"

Paul walked quickly over to the door. He turned back and shook his head.

"Great!" Asa exclaimed. "You leave messages on your answering machine and your front door. Anybody who wanted to could probably find you at any given moment. Just great!"

"You said Mr. Grimsley was killed," Sarah said quietly. "The man who drowned?"

"What happened to him, Sarah," Asa said bluntly, "was that he was shot and thrown into the river."

"Oh no." Sarah caught Paul's arm. She felt a sudden light-headedness, as if she'd been playing ball in the sun too long and needed to sit down.

"Are you all right, Sarah?" he asked, sliding his arm around her shoulder.

"Yes. No. How could anybody hurt that old man?"

Asa glared at Sarah. Hurt that old man. She had to be the most trusting soul in the world. She flitted through life, assuming nobody meant her any harm, that everybody was as kind and innocent as she. Now life was shattering her innocence and he couldn't do anything to stop it.

"He's a swindler, Sarah," Asa said. "His last address was the federal pen. And he made some interesting friends in there, ones who thought he had a thumb too many."

Snow Sims let out a deep sigh. "Any ideas, Canyon?"

"My guess is that Grimsley knew something that somebody wanted to know. The missing thumb has all the markings of torture. The men who did that could be the same group that ripped up this place."

Sarah shivered. She didn't want to believe that that kind of criminal mind had invaded her safe little town. Of course there were drugs, and sometimes a man would get drunk and beat up his wife on Saturday night. Occasionally more violent crimes took place. But this came from the outside and that frightened Sarah.

Asa walked over and took Sarah's hand, pulling her forward into the light. "Where is it, Sarah?"

"The safe? At home, in the loft. Why? Do

you think—Mother and Robert! Oh, Asa, you don't think anybody would hurt them?"

Sims quickly flicked on his two-way phone and directed the nearest cars to the old Wilson place. He instructed them to check out both the house and the barn and to remain there until he arrived.

Asa helped Paul lock up the shop and then got into Sarah's van with her, making sure one of the officers followed in his truck. They fell in behind Paul, blue lights flashing.

The Wilson house was surrounded with Smyrna police cars in a matter of minutes. But, apart from having alarmed Sarah's mother and stepfather, everything seemed to be in order. After a thorough look around Sims and his officers were dispatched back to town. Any further needs would have to be supplied by the county police, under whose jurisdiction the Wilson property fell.

After they'd all gone Asa followed Sarah upstairs, closing and locking the door leading down to the basketball court. He turned to Sarah.

"Now, let's see it."

"The safe?"

"The safe."

Sarah led him across the loft to the unfinished room in front of the hayloft doors. The long, narrow space had been turned into a storage area and workroom. It was filled with books, a desk, and assorted pieces of sports equipment. The safe was sitting on a table beneath a gooseneck lamp.

Asa studied the small lead safe. He raised his eyebrows, glancing at Sarah skeptically. "This is it?"

"That's it. It appears to be some kind of wall safe, perhaps the kind that a European woman might have used to keep her jewels in."

"Made in Europe, huh. Any idea where?"

"My guess would be Germany, but I can't be certain. There seems to be some similarity between the lock and the works of a particular clock maker in the seventeenth century."

"How do you know that?"

"By studying some of Pop's antique books. He collected information on locks and doors that date back to the 1600s. I just haven't been able to hit on the right combination to get it open."

"Can it be forced?"

"Maybe, but it could destroy the contents and Mr. Grimsley was insistent that the safe not be harmed."

"Mr. Grimsley no longer has a say, Sarah. Can you open it? No, never mind, Sarah, I'll just take it to the station." He started to lift the safe.

"Asa, I'm the best locksmith in the county. If anybody can open this safe without destroying it, it's me. Let me do it for you."

Asa took a long look at Sarah. Didn't she realize the potential danger? It was becoming clear that a man was dead because of this safe and Asa didn't intend to let the killers' search for it go any further. The sooner the press printed the fact that the safe had been found—and he'd make certain that it did—the sooner Sarah would be safe. "Don't be foolish, Sarah. I won't put you in danger."

"I see. Always in charge. Always the one to decide. If this is the way you treated Jeanie I'm not surprised that she eloped with Mike without talking it over with you."

Asa blanched.

Sarah sucked in a surprised breath.

There was a long, tense silence.

"All right, Sarah. We need the safe opened. Open it. But I want you to stay here, with your door locked. Leave the answering machine on so that you can tell who's calling and don't answer unless it's me."

"Anything else, *sir*?" She gave a sharp salute.

"Yes!" he yelled. "Open the damn safe before I get back!"

"I intend to."

Sarah walked out into the living quarters. Just as she reached the door a hand caught her shoulder and swung her around.

"Sarah Wilson, I don't know what you think you're doing, but I know what I'm doing. I'm protecting the woman I love whether she wants me to or not."

With that, Asa planted a rough kiss on her lips, strode down the stairs out the door, and slammed it behind him. "Lock this door!"

Woodenly Sarah followed him downstairs and locked the outer door. Her lips were still stinging from the force of Asa's kiss, her heart still racing from its power. The woman I love?

She picked up a basketball and made a few practice shots absentmindedly before she returned to the loft and slid the deadbolt in place.

The woman I love.

She knew the admission hadn't come easily. She wasn't even sure he knew what he'd said.

Tomorrow he'd probably deny it. Tomorrow he'd probably be gone.

Being with Asa had become so necessary to her life that she couldn't imagine how she'd ever lived before she met him, or would exist if he left. She'd been so absorbed with this strong, silent man that she'd let everything else fall into second place. If she'd paid attention to her job and opened the safe to begin with, Mr. Grimsley might not be dead. But now Mr. Grimsley was gone and she might be the only one able to find a link to his killers.

She turned on the light and settled down with her father's books. The combination had to be in there somewhere. All she had to do was find it.

An hour later she stopped for a sandwich and a quick shower before returning to her task. She glanced out the window and saw a dark car parked beneath the pine trees. Asa was having her watched. The knowledge gave her a quick thrill until she decided that it was as much police procedure as personal concern.

By midnight she'd become completely frustrated. If the face of the lock had readable numbers she'd be a lot closer to solving the puzzle. All she had to go on was a series of lines that marked the exterior of the safe into squares and a lock that defied understanding. Rubik's Cube had not been as unsolvable.

Just as she was ready to give up and let Asa have the safe she heard a faint scraping sound outside the barn. She turned off the lights and tiptoed to the hayloft doors, giving Asa a silent thank you for oiling the hinges as she cracked them and peeked out.

She could see a man in front of her downstairs door working at the lock. *He's trying to break in,* she realized.

Asa was right. Somebody had traced the safe to her. Anxiously she peered out at the car, wondering how she could get the attention of whoever was sitting inside. But why hadn't the intruder already been spotted? That's why the car was there, wasn't it? Maybe not. Maybe the car belonged to the gang.

Quickly Sarah made her way to the phone. She'd call Asa. He'd know what to do.

There was no dial tone. The phone was dead.

Up to now Sarah had been intrigued. But this was serious. If the man got inside there was no way that she could get away. The stairs were the only way out. Except for the metal grate. It hoisted furniture; it ought to hold her.

As quietly as possible Sarah put the safe on the grate. She got her purse and keys and waited until she heard the intruder enter the barn below. It would take him a minute to figure out what was there.

Opening the hayloft doors wide, she could see from the play of his flashlight that he was inside. Sarah took a deep breath and lifted the grate from the floor, swinging it outside the loft. She would lower herself to the ground like a platter of dirty dishes in a dumbwaiter. *Thanks Pop, for the escape hatch,* she said silently, as she climbed on.

The grate groaned and jerked as she began her descent. It shimmied, then hit the side of the barn with a thump. As she steadied the grate she heard an oath. She'd been discovered. The intruder raced outside, reaching the ground before she did. He stood, waiting for her, an insidious smile on his face.

"Miss Wilson, I presume?"

"Who are you?"

"Let's just say that we have a mutual friend. He couldn't come, so I'm here in his place. Is that the safe?"

He leaped up, catching the corner of the grate in one hand, making it rock unsteadily.

"Stop that," Sarah called out. "This house is being watched. You'd better go if you don't want to end up in jail."

"You mean the man in the car? He's taking a nap. I don't think that you're likely to wake him."

Sarah groaned. She was in for it now. Asa had warned her about leaving messages on her answering machine. He'd told her not to leave the barn, too. Not only had she disobeyed him, but she was about to lose the safe. Unless . . . She began to rock the grate back and forth as she lowered herself.

The man's attempts to reach the grate made it sway even more. But Sarah hadn't taken the fence into account. The grate hit one of the posts and tilted. The safe slid off, banged against the post, and careened off, slamming into the man who was trying to reach it. He crumpled to the ground in a heap against the gate.

Sarah quickly let the grate to the ground and got off. She stooped down beside the man and placed her fingertips against the side of his neck, checking for a pulse. He wasn't dead, but there was a lump on the side of his head where he'd hit the post. Apparently he was just unconscious, but for how long?

She ran back upstairs for the handcuffs she'd intended to give Asa. She fitted them around the burglar's wrists, clamped the burglar to the post, and stepped back to survey her work.

Certain that the intruder was secure, she made her way to the patrol car. Inside, his head sprawled against the back of the seat, was Paul Martin.

Sarah shook him. He didn't respond. Oh, God. He'd been hurt trying to protect her. Quickly, she ran toward her mother's house, her heart in her throat. The doors were locked as usual. She'd left her keys on the grate and was forced to ring the bell.

After several peals the porch light came on and the door opened.

"Sarah?"

Her stepfather was holding his pistol. "What's wrong, Sarah?"

"There's been an accident. I need to use your phone." She pushed past him, picked up the receiver, and dialed 911. When the operator came on the line Sarah requested an ambulance, then asked that Deputy Asa Canyon of the sheriff's office be notified.

After she explained what had happened to her mother and Robert she hurried back to check on Paul. By that time he was beginning to stir.

"Paul, are you all right?"

"Sarah? What's going on?"

"Apparently the burglar knocked you cold."

He stepped out of the car, grabbed his head, and slumped back against the car. "Ah, Sarah. I'm sorry. Where is he?"

"I've got him handcuffed to the gate post. Here, you'd better have the keys."

The sound of sirens broke the silence as Asa's truck, followed by an ambulance and a sheriff's car, came roaring up the drive and screeched to a stop.

Asa didn't call out or stop moving until he reached Sarah's side and put his hands on her shoulders. He stood, silent, searching her face until he was satisfied that she wasn't hurt. Then he stepped back and let out a deep ragged sigh. "What happened?"

Sarah explained as Paul handed the ambulance attendant the handcuff keys and walked up next to Asa, who was blinking in amazement. "Maybe you'd better sign her up for the sheriff's department, Asa. She can handle herself pretty good."

"She'd never make it as a deputy," Asa said sharply. "She doesn't follow orders." He went over to where the medics were loading the criminal into the ambulance. He needed to put space between himself and Sarah. When he'd got the word that there was someone breaking into her house he'd almost gone wild. Asa knew that he was a strong man, but it took every ounce of strength he could muster not to take her in his arms and shake her.

"Don't pay any attention to him, Sarah," Paul commented under his breath. "He's just worried."

"Get in the ambulance, Paul," Asa instructed. "You need to let the doctors have a look at you."

"But what about Sarah?"

"My guess is that she won't be harmed now that she's opened the safe."

"Opened?" Sarah dashed over to the safe. It *was* open. Apparently the safe had hit the post at exactly the right spot to spring it open. From a small lead box inside a sheaf of paper money was spilling out.

"Money?" Paul asked in disbelief. "There really was money in there."

Asa picked up the bills and slapped them on his thigh. "Yep, Confederate money, lots of

Confederate money, I'd say. You think the South's gonna rise again?"

Sarah couldn't believe what Asa was saying. "You mean that Mr. Grimsley was killed for a safe filled with Confederate money?"

"Looks like it. I can't see anything else in there." They walked back toward the ambulance. Asa and Sarah watched as Paul climbed inside and the driver started the engine.

"Canyon, I'll put the word out to the press that a Civil War safe was found, filled with paper money. That ought to call off any of your burglar's friends."

Asa nodded as the ambulance pulled off down the drive, leaving him and Sarah standing by the apple trees.

"So, it's over," Sarah said quietly. "What about Mr. Grimsley?"

"We'll know more after I talk to the intruder," Asa explained. "But my guess is that Grimsley saw the newspaper article about the house and bragged to the wrong people about the legendary safe. He got out of prison first and came looking for it."

"Because of the restoration going on, he managed to find it, when nobody else had ever been able to before."

"Yes, and his friend was right behind."

Sarah shivered. "But why kill him?"

"Who knows? Maybe the friend thought he knew where the safe was and didn't want to share the contents."

"That seems such a waste. A murder over a

safe filled with Confederate money." Feeling numb, Sarah started toward the barn.

"Sarah?"

She swallowed hard but didn't turn around. "Yes?"

"Are you all right?"

"Yes."

"I'm sorry I yelled at you. I warned you that I didn't know much about being nice."

"Yes, you did."

"I—I'd stay with you, but I want to go to the hospital and get a statement from your burglar."

"I understand. You have a job to do. At least you're doing yours. I didn't."

"Of course you did. Grimsley wanted the safe open, it's open."

Asa wasn't coming any nearer. She hadn't expected him to get out of the truck the first time he'd seen the barn, but he had. Yet tonight he wasn't following her.

Sarah replaced the safe on the grate and raised it to the open hayloft doors, then fastened the rope on a nail on the wall. She stopped at the door and asked, "Will you let me know what the doctors say about Paul? I don't want to think that he got hurt because of me."

"Sure. Will you be here?"

"I'm a permanent person, Asa. I'll be here. I promise."

Sure you will. But he didn't say it. He only walked away. At the gate he stopped and spoke to Sarah's mother.

"Will you check on her later, Asa?" Alice

asked. "She's much too trusting and independent for her own good. I worry about her."

"I'll send another car to stand guard," Asa promised. "I didn't want to concern her. I think the man we have in custody was working alone, or someone would have been with him. But we can't be sure until I talk to him."

"You're a good man, Asa Canyon," Alice said.

"No, I'm not, but I think that I'm learning."

On the way to the hospital Asa radioed a call for a surveillance car to be sent to Sarah's house. He didn't have any indication that there was likely to be more trouble, but he just wanted to play it safe.

The doctor at the hospital said that Officer Martin was fine. The man Sarah had captured was suffering from a concussion and was still unconscious. He was expected to come to at any time and if Asa wanted to question him, he'd better stand by.

Asa talked a nurse into providing a cup of decent coffee and settled down to wait. It was nearly two o'clock. He closed his eyes. Might as well try for a nap.

Knowing Sarah Wilson was both calming and exhausting. One way or another she managed to keep him awake all night, either by intruding in his life or his dreams. There seemed to be no way to shut her out.

He sighed and thought about her wide, open smile and about her contention that he was a nice man. And he decided that perhaps nice was like beauty. It was in the eyes of the beholder. To Sarah, he was nice. Maybe that was enough.

Eight

Sarah couldn't help but think of Mr. Grimsley. She could still see his fear, feel his desperation in wanting her to open the safe. He had been so concerned about its contents. It didn't seem fair that he'd lost his life over something so worthless as Confederate money.

But life wasn't fair. It didn't seem fair that she'd lost her father, or that she'd fallen in love with a man who was determined not to love her back. She wasn't even sure when she knew that she loved him. Perhaps it had been in her heart since that night at the lake, and it had waited quietly for her recognition.

In a moment of stress Asa had admitted that he loved her. But he certainly didn't seem happy about it. And she was afraid she'd never be able to convince him that she wasn't going to be one of those temporary people in his life.

She closed the downstairs doors, making certain that the lock was secure. Then she went upstairs and locked the door to her living quarters. Once inside, she pulled up the grate and locked those doors. The barn was secure, though she didn't know whether she was keeping someone out, or keeping herself in.

Something about the safe caught at her emotions. It was broken, its small door hanging from one corner. At least she could put it back together. If she fixed something, she might feel better. She placed the safe on the table and switched on the light. Pulling up a chair, she studied the small lead box, trying to decide why it had been so difficult to open.

Then she saw what she'd missed before. The open door wasn't where she'd expected. It had been intricately placed within the engraved lines that made up the outer squares. Nobody would notice it because of the design. Sarah realized the lock was operated by application of pressure. The combination lock was a red herring, meant to fool anyone trying to open the safe. She could have worked on that lock from now to next year with no results.

In the process of returning the door to its proper mounting she felt a tiny indentation just inside the opening. She pressed it. A drawer beneath the door slid open. A secret compartment. Could this be what Mr. Grimsley had been searching for? To still her rapidly beating heart Sarah took a long deep breath. Inside the tiny drawer was a folded slip of yellowed paper.

Sarah started toward the phone, anxious to share her discovery with Asa. Then she remembered the phone was out. She'd show it to him tomorrow when he came by. No, he needed to know now. The paper might be important. She'd take it to him. But he'd told her not to leave. The last time she'd disobeyed him she'd almost been caught. This time she'd follow orders.

But she had to know what Mr. Grimsley had been looking for. Surely Asa would understand that.

Carefully she removed the paper from the drawer and unfolded it on the table. Pulling the lamp closer she studied what appeared to be an architectural drawing. The lines were faded, the writing almost illegible, but it was a map of some kind. There was a house on one half of the paper, and a room that looked almost like a reflection in a mirror. A wall behind a wall?

The second half of the page was less understandable. It seemed to be a trail or a tunnel leading to a second building. Something about the second building looked familiar. There was a drawing of an intricate carving over the door, giving the suggestion of an animal.

A lion. That symbol was part of the ornate design over the door of the old Bank of Smyrna building. And the house in the drawing had to be the Grimsley house. This was what Lincoln Grimsley was after. The drawing showed a tunnel from the Grimsley house to the bank and beyond to the railroad.

Underground Railroad? Had the Grimsley house and the bank been part of the Underground Railroad during the days of slavery? Or had the tunnel been set up to allow the banker to escape with his gold? Perhaps no one would ever know. All that had been passed down apparently was this map.

She took it into the kitchen, where she continued to study it as she served herself a wedge of the apple pie she hadn't gotten a chance to serve Asa for dinner. Its cinnamon fragrance made her think of Asa, and how much sharper her sense of smell, and taste, and touch had become since he came into her life.

Her mother had told her that she had to teach him to love. How was that possible when she didn't know how? There was no question about their bodies being right for each other, but what about themselves as people? Asa was strong, hard, the Lone Ranger, wearing a mask as he rescued damsels in distress and disappeared into the sunset. She was more like silly putty, adapting herself to the situation and the person she was with according to need.

How could they possibly find a common ground?

How could she do without him, now that she knew what it was to love a man? It was more than just responding to someone in pain who needed her. Asa was strength. He was forever and she needed that kind of anchor. In her most private moments she knew that part of her giving was because giving satisfied an emptiness inside her. That emptiness was gone now that Asa had filled it.

She took a bite of the pie and reached inside a kitchen drawer for her magnifying glass. It wasn't there. It had to be somewhere. She finally located it in the bathroom cabinet. Maybe Asa was right. Maybe she ought to organize her cabinets better. She'd wasted valuable time.

The magnifying glass brought the faint lines into better focus. As she followed the path of the tunnel she realized with startling clarity where it led. Not just to the bank but, if she interpreted the drawing right, straight into the vault.

Lincoln Grimsley wasn't looking for money in the safe. He was looking for the tunnel to the bank vault. He and the intruder she'd captured had planned to rob the bank. Suppose these two weren't the only ones involved? Sarah brushed aside any concern about not following orders. She carefully folded the map and, gathering her keys, made her way outside to Henry.

After giving a brief thought to stopping at the house to call Asa, she decided not to wake her folks again. She'd stop at the first public phone.

She'd just check out the bank first. If the man she'd conked on the head wasn't the only member of the gang, the others might already be destroying the house or the bank, or worse. Asa might have questioned the injured man and found out what she knew. Asa! He could be in real danger.

"Oh, Asa," she uttered in fear, "please be all right."

If she hadn't been so caught up in worrying about Asa, she would have been more careful about leaving the barn. She might have realized that someone was following her. The car didn't show itself until she pulled into the parking lot of the bank. The two men who jumped out and dragged her from the van were carrying guns and they were very serious about getting inside the bank. Sarah was a locksmith. She was better than the treasure map they'd been searching for.

The intensive care unit sounded like a hundred machines whirring in unison. Asa glanced around and shivered. Death was one part of his job that he'd never had a stomach for. He'd been nineteen in Vietnam when his commanding officer had died saving Asa. The memory still slipped inside his dreams and reminded him that death was waiting for him. Since then the morgue and the hospital were about as close as he wanted to come.

The man's eyes were closed. His arms had needles and tubes attached to them. Asa could see that he was breathing, but the movement of his chest was shallow. Asa was told that his vital signs were good, but he was still unconscious.

The hospital workers were wrong.

At the sound of Asa's boots on the tiled floor, the man's eyes flew open. A look of resignation passed over his face and he sighed.

"Did you get Fred and Lennie?"

Asa felt his heart sink. He'd hoped that there was only this man and Lincoln Grimsley.

"Yes. What did you hope to accomplish? All this for a safe full of Confederate money."

"Then there was no treasure map."

"What made you think there would be?"

"That bragging old fool. I should have known that cock-and-bull story about a secret way to get inside the bank was phony. What'd Fred and Lennie do? Get tired of waiting and bust in? That sounds like something they'd do."

The bank? What is the fool talking about? "No," Asa said. "The truth is, until you told me, I wasn't sure there was a Fred and Lennie. Now that I know that much, why don't you tell me the rest of it?"

"What's it worth to me?"

Asa took a step closer to the bed and leaned over the man. "It's worth your life. You tried to hurt somebody that I care about. You trashed her shop and you would have hurt her, just as I'm going to hurt you, if you don't tell me everything."

"But—" Fear welled up in the bedridden man. "But you're an officer of the law."

"Yes, but first I'm a man, a man you don't want to make any more angry than he already is."

The criminal began to talk.

Ten minutes later Asa was on his way to Smyrna Village. He put in a call to Snow Sims, instructing him to meet him at the bank. He was too late. When he got there, a car and a van, a red van with a smiley face, were already parked outside.

Where was she? His heart sunk.

The door to the bank wasn't locked. Sarah had to be inside. But why? He'd radioed for another surveillance car to watch her house. How could she have gotten away? Unless the back-up didn't get to her barn in time to stop her. Why hadn't she stayed put? Why had she come here?

Asa drew his gun and pushed the door open, sliding silently inside. He could hear male voices in the back, behind the tellers' cages and the offices. He followed the sound, hoping beyond hope that he wouldn't find Sarah trying to rescue someone from somebody.

Then he saw her in the beam of a flashlight. She was standing beside the vault, her toolbox open on the floor beside her. Two men were standing over her. It was obvious that Sarah was being instructed to open the vault.

Had she disregarded his instructions and come here on her own, or had she been brought?

One of the criminals was holding a gun. From the intruder's descriptions, Asa guessed this one was Fred. His desperate expression told Asa that he'd better do something and quick. They'd already killed one man and Asa was certain that they were jumpy enough to kill again.

"All right, girl," Lennie said. "One more time. Are you going to open this vault, or do we give you a little swimming lesson like we gave your old friend, Lincoln?"

"I've already told you that I never saw Lincoln Grimsley before he came into my shop. And the safe he wanted me to open only contained a lot of Confederate money. The man who broke in my house will verify that I'm telling the truth."

"Yeah, and where is he?"

"He's in the hospital. He was injured, trying to steal the safe."

"Listen, girl," Lennie said menacingly. "I don't know what you're trying to pull but we don't believe you. Crackerman wouldn't have let himself get caught. You did something to him. The way to get into the bank vault was inside that safe, Lincoln swore. Why else would you be here? You must have found the combination."

"Sorry, men," Sarah said, in what she hoped was a convincing voice. "There was no combination. You killed that old man for nothing."

"Then it won't matter much if we kill you for the same reason, lady," Fred said in a voice that seemed even more deadly than Lennie's.

Sarah let out a nervous laugh. Why hadn't she followed Asa's instructions? Why hadn't she waited for him to return and give him the map? Because she'd been worried about him. And that worry had overruled her better judgment.

Lennie stepped back. "What's so funny, girl?"

"Nothing. It's just that there's no way I could open this vault, if I wanted to. It has a time release on it that's operated by a computer. Only the bank president and another bank officer can override the controls and they aren't here."

"Then you better find another way because we intend to get into that vault." Fred pressed the barrel of the gun against Sarah's cheek.

She gasped. She didn't want to die. Not now, not when Asa had come into her life.

In the shadows Asa considered his options. Sarah was telling the truth, but they wouldn't believe it. Sooner or later it was going to occur to one of them that she was no use to them. Everything was falling apart. They'd already killed once. Asa couldn't allow them to kill again. He had to do something now.

"I'm the bank president," Asa called out, and stepped into the room. "What's the meaning of this?"

"Asa—"

"Do not, I repeat, do not open your mouth, Sarah Wilson," Asa said with the threat of murder in his voice.

"Well, well," Lennie said. "The bank president, eh? Then you're just the man we need." He made his way to the front door and looked outside for a long time before turning back to Asa. "What are you doing here?"

"I left something in my office, and I came by to pick it up."

"So, if you're the president, open this vault."

"I can't, and even if I could, I wouldn't."

"I don't much think you're in a position to bargain," Fred said, leveling his gun at Asa.

"Oh, but I am. There is no way that the vault can be opened until 9 A.M."

"We don't believe you," Lennie said, his voice growing more agitated. "This woman is a locksmith. She's already admitted that she opened Lincoln's safe. She can open this one. Maybe she needs some persuasion. You her boyfriend?"

"I'm her friend, yes."

"I thought so from the way you looked at each other." Lennie reached inside his coat and pulled out his gun, aiming it at Asa. "Maybe you'd like to keep each other from getting shot?"

Sarah felt her heart contract. *Not Asa. Asa couldn't die. She couldn't stop her father, but she could stop this.* She opened her mouth and tried to speak, but no words came. "No!" she finally screamed, reaching out and jostling Lennie just as he pulled the trigger. A muted sound pierced the silence. The bullet found its target—Asa's shoulder.

A spurt of blood circled the bullet hole as Sarah gasped. For the first time in her life, Sarah felt a raging anger toward another human being. No amount of money in any vault was worth Asa's life.

"Wait!" she screamed in desperation. "I don't have the combination, but I know how to get into the vault."

"How?" Fred was suspicious.

"Come with me." Sarah whirled around and started toward the front door.

The bank robbers were too startled for a second to stop her. Then Fred realized what was happening and followed.

"Hold on, girl," Lennie barked. "Where do you think you're going?"

"I'm going to show you another way to get into the vault. Mr. Grimsley's safe didn't contain the combination, but it had something just as good. If you two want to get inside that vault, you'd better follow me and you'd better do it quick."

"She's lying!" Asa's voice thundered. "You don't need her. This is my bank and I'm the only one who can open this safe. You're just wasting time. If you want to get inside where the real money is, you'll have to work with me."

The sound of sirens in the distance cut through the talk. The lights of the patrol cars flashed on the wall through the glass front door. Fred whipped around. "Ah, hell. Sounds like the whole force out there."

Lennie shifted from one foot to the other. "We'd better get out of here."

"We can't," Fred said, as the sirens died and doors began to open and close. "There are too many of them."

"I can get you out of here," Asa said. "Let the lady go and I'll arrange for the manager to come in. Together we can open the vault."

"Why?"

"Because I don't want to bleed to death in a standoff. The money's insured and I don't want to die. It's the only choice you have. Take it or leave it."

The two men looked at each other desperately. "All right," Fred agreed. "But remember, we've killed one man and we can kill you too. The electric chair doesn't keep count."

Sarah glanced at Asa, who was standing ramrod stiff. The circle of blood on his shoulder was widening. "I won't go without you," Sarah said. "If you stay, so do I."

"Sorry, Sarah. I travel alone. I told you that in the beginning. Nothing's changed." Asa could see that she had no intention of going along with his plan. He had to do something. "Sarah, I lied. Jeanie was the most important thing in my life. She still is, not you."

He tried not to see Sarah wince. He only hoped he could convince her that he was serious; otherwise she'd do something foolish.

"You were something new, a nice diversion for a while," he added in a rush. "But Jeanie won't stay with Mike. She'll come back. She always has."

"I don't believe you," Sarah countered softly.

"Lady, we don't have time for dramatics," Fred said, and caught her by the shoulder. "From where I stand, having the bank president as a hostage looks fine. You're just in the way." He cracked the door and with a quick motion, pushed her through it, yelling, "Hold your fire, cops!"

Paul Martin ran up the sidewalk in a crouch and dropped beside Sarah. "You okay?"

"Yes, I'm fine, but they've got Asa. He's been shot."

"Damn! Let's get you out of here."

They ran back toward the circle of police cars to a safe spot where Sarah explained the situation. Captain Sims listened, then began issuing orders. As he reached for the bullhorn so that he could communicate with the robbers, Sarah grabbed a flashlight and motioned for Paul to follow her.

"Where are we going, Sarah?"

"To get Asa."

Sarah moved quickly across the street to the Grimsley house, broke a pane in the door and slipped her hand inside to open it.

Paul whispered uneasily, "What are you doing, Sarah?"

"I'm getting us into the vault. Do you have your gun?"

She turned on the flashlight and played it

across the room at a far wall. According to the diagram it had to be that wall that hid the entrance to a second room. She walked up to it, pressing, knocking. When she came to the panel by the fireplace she heard the hollow sound she'd been searching for. The entrance was behind the wall, but how to get there?

The fireplace. She played her hands along the bricks, feeling, testing. If Mr. Grimsley's safe opened on a pressure combination, maybe the entrance to the tunnel operated the same way.

But nothing was happening. Could she be wrong? Could the tunnel have been discovered and dismantled years ago? Just as she was about to give up, a panel in the hearth slid open, revealing a narrow passageway beneath. Sarah sat down on the floor and slid into the narrow black gap.

"Wait, Sarah." Paul tried to follow but couldn't. "The opening is too narrow. I can't get inside."

Sarah shined the flashlight along the crude tunnel. It was obvious that nobody had used it in years. Only because the walls were brick had it lasted.

"Sarah, you'd better take my gun," Paul said in a loud whisper.

"No thanks. I wouldn't know how to use it if I did. Go back to Captain Sims and tell him that, with any luck, I'm going to get into the bank behind them. I'll cause a disturbance of some kind, so he should be ready to come in quick. Tell him to keep a lot of noise going so the crooks won't hear me. Then come back and see if you can make this opening larger in case, well, just in case."

Sarah took a deep breath of fresh air and turned back to the tunnel. She didn't like small, dark places. She didn't like spiders. She didn't like rats and she had a feeling that she was facing all three.

Whoever had built the tunnel intended for it to last, and except in a few spots, the shoring was still holding. It had survived the shelling of Atlanta during the Civil War and was withstanding the construction of the parking lot overhead.

Cautiously Sarah picked her way forward. She didn't for one minute believe all that nonsense Asa spewed out about Jeanie. He was trying to protect her and she loved him for it. She couldn't tell how badly he was hurt because he never let anybody know about his pain. But she knew she had to get to him right away.

After a few minutes that seemed like hours she reached an intersection. What looked like some rough steps led off to the right. Straight ahead was a wall of loose dirt where the roof of the tunnel had collapsed. Sarah said a silent prayer that the steps would take her into the bank. Relying totally on her memory of the drawing now, for the flashlight battery was weakening, she put one foot on the first step and began to search for an exit.

The air was very stale and she began to feel almost light-headed. If she didn't get out soon she could very well faint. That wouldn't happen, she vowed, forcing herself to take quick little breaths and holding them in as long as possible.

She took two more steps that ended at a door, a very old door with the handle on her side. *Please open.* She caught hold of the handle and pulled. It didn't move. She groaned. To come this far and not be able to get in . . . No, she wouldn't accept that. Frantically she flicked the light up and down the door, until she saw the problem. An iron beam had fallen across the door, effectively blocking it.

Sarah tried to lift the beam, but time and pressure had wedged it in place. She finally found a loose brick in the wall, and by using it as a hammer, she was able to force the rail up. She didn't know how long she took. She could only hope the robbers hadn't heard her pounding.

She took hold of the handle and pulled again. The warped door resisted stubbornly. She pulled harder. She wasn't about to give up now. She'd get through. She had to.

She gave the door one last desperate jerk. It opened a crack. Then the crack widened and she found herself in what appeared to be a closet instead of the vault.

No, she was in a small washroom. But where? Cautiously she crept forward in the darkness, until she came to a wall. By following it she found another door and turned the knob.

The bank manager's office. She could hear the murmur of voices beyond the half-open door. Taking a long, deep breath of fresh air, Sarah moved forward.

Peering out, she could see that Fred and Lennie were standing beside the front door, watching the outside activity. Asa was slumped in one of the chairs in the lobby as though he'd passed out. His hands were tied. Though he appeared to be very weak, she figured that his condition was likely a pose meant to lull his captors into a false sense of security.

Glancing around, Sarah studied the situation. What she needed was a way to create a distraction. Then she saw it—a round brass paperweight on the desk behind her. She hadn't been a star ballplayer all her life for nothing.

Slipping through the door she made her way silently to a spot just behind Asa. Drawing back, she took aim and threw the brass ball. She watched it sail through the door. Amidst the shattering of glass panes, she called out, "Asa!"

"What the—" Lennie began firing at the police.

Asa instantly came to his feet. Sarah grabbed him and led him to the office. Just as they reached the washroom, Sarah heard Fred's voice. "After him, he's getting away!"

"Where are we going?" Asa growled.

"Caving! Shut up and follow me!"

She shoved him through the hidden wall

panel, followed, and pushed the beam back across the door.

They leaned against the door in the darkness, hardly breathing for fear of discovery.

"He's gone. Where'd he go?" they heard Lennie ask.

"Hell, I don't know. He just vanished. Maybe he got into that vault."

Sarah exhaled in a long jerky sigh. Moisture filled her eyes and spilled over on her cheeks. "Asa?" she managed to whisper. "Are you all right?"

"I'll survive." His voice, though low, was harsh and cold. "Do you know what a chance you just took?"

"Me? You were the one who got shot," she replied, making her way down the steps.

"You knew that they had a gun and you came back into the bank like you think you're invincible."

"Sorry. I suppose I should have let you stay and get your thumb cut off too."

"Untie me, Sarah."

"Why? So you can go back inside and get yourself killed? Forget it."

"Then I'll do it myself."

Asa began to work at the crude rope as he followed Sarah through the tunnel. Her flashlight died halfway back and they had to walk in the dark, feeling their way along the wall. Sarah knew that she must look like a chimney sweep. Her face felt gritty from wiping the tears away with hands that were covered with dust and grime. She fell a couple of times and skinned her knees and her ankle stung where something had scratched her.

When she reached the entrance to the Grimsley house she stopped. There was nothing behind her but silence. She'd concentrated so hard on getting to the end that she'd failed to make sure Asa had kept up with her. Maybe Asa was hurt worse than she'd thought and had fainted. She whirled around and began to run back down the tunnel when she collided with a rock-hard object—unyielding, immovable, and familiar.

"Asa," she whispered, "are you all right?"

"Yes," he said, putting his now freed arms around her and leaning against her for a long, sweet moment. "I should have known that you'd come back. You told me that you weren't one of those temporary people."

"I'll always be here, Asa. If you need me."

His grip began to loosen and Sarah thought that he was pulling away again, just as he did every time they came together. Then he added in a weak voice, "I never thought I'd say it Sarah. But I think I do."

He slid to the ground, unconscious.

"The bullet went through his shoulder," the doctor was saying. "He just lost a lot of blood. Any other man would be flat on his back in intensive care."

Sarah took a look at Asa and thought that was where he ought to be, instead of sitting on the edge of the examining table in the emergency room. She was still in shock. When Asa had passed out, she'd screamed. Paul Martin had pulled up the flooring and jumped inside to help get Asa out. On the way to the hospital, Paul explained how the two robbers had been apprehended, thanks to Sarah's help.

The doctor put the last piece of tape on the bandage and stepped back. "Okay, Deputy, if you're determined to leave, that ought to hold you. I've had the nurse arrange for you to have enough antibiotics and tablets for pain to get you through the night. I'll want to check this tomorrow."

"Fine." Asa came unsteadily to his feet, steeled himself to walk, and moved out of the cubicle past Sarah. At the door he stopped and turned back to her.

"Let's go home, lady, before I collapse and embarrass myself in front of all these people."

A wide smile appeared on Sarah's face as she took the two steps to Asa's side. "Are you sure?" she asked, sliding her arm around his waist.

"No, but let's say I'm willing to talk about it."

Yet they didn't talk that night. Sarah took Asa to the barn, gave him his medication, and put him to bed. He was asleep before she could comment on the navy blue briefs he was wearing. He was safe and that was all that mattered. With a heart filled with joy she took off her clothes and slid in beside him. If he woke in pain during the night, she'd be there to share it.

Epilogue

They spent almost all day in the woods looking before Sarah spotted it.

"There, I knew it was here somewhere.
That's the one."

"Are you sure? That tree looks like it ought
to go on the governor's front lawn."

"That's it. Pop and I spotted it years ago and
we saved it for a special occasion. I wanted to
cut it the last Christmas he lived, but he said
no. Now I know what we were saving it for."

Asa caught Sarah in his arms and planted a
kiss on her lips. "For me?"

"For us. For our first Christmas."

Asa cut the tree and dragged it to the van.
He had to trim eight inches from the bottom
so it wouldn't drag on the ground as they
drove down the dirt road to her place.

The lake beyond the barn was filling nicely.
And the foundation for the house overlooking

it was laid out, ready for construction to begin.

"Oh, Asa." Sarah sighed and moved into his embrace as soon as they'd stopped and gotten out of the van. "If anyone had told me a year ago that I'd be married now I wouldn't have believed them."

"I know," he said quietly. "I still pinch myself every morning. Speaking of being surprised, you should have heard Jeanie yell when I told her."

"Jeanie?"

"Yes, she called this morning. She and Mike are on their way to Arizona, where his family lives."

"How is she?"

"She seems very happy. She's going to have a baby."

"Oh?" Sarah felt her breath quicken. Asa had been outspoken about not having children. He didn't seem to want close friends, or family either. He was so afraid that something might come between the two of them. Sarah was worried. She'd suspected the truth for several weeks before she'd learned that in spite of their best efforts, she was pregnant.

"Mike is beside himself," Asa was saying. "He's even agreed to take a job with his father's company, and Jeanie is going to retire for a while. I never thought any of that would happen."

They dragged the tree to the barn and lowered the grate. Sarah ran upstairs to guide the tree into the loft as Asa operated the pulley. After several false starts they changed positions. Finally the tree was inside the loft and Asa secured it to the floor with two-by-fours and guy wires.

"There," he said. "But I don't know how you expect to decorate it. We'll have to use a stepladder."

"Probably," she agreed. "But after it's done, we'll open the doors and just think how beautiful it will look to anyone passing by. It fills the space as if it was meant to be here."

"Just like me," Asa said. "There was no room for me anywhere until you took me in."

"Shall we decorate it tonight?"

"Later," Asa said, in a low voice. "Right now I need you to love me, Sarah. I need to feel you around me, to be the other part of me."

"Oh, Asa, I am. I'll always be a part of you."

Every time they'd made love in the three months they'd been married, Sarah had marveled at the wonder of Asa's need for her. Instead of lessening, it grew. Instead of reaching a saturation point, it seemed that every glance, every look, every touch made them more aware of this wonderful thing that existed between them.

It was very late when they pulled on their robes and finally finished placing the last ornament on the tree. "All we need now," Asa said with satisfaction, "is the star. Where is it, Sarah?"

Sarah glanced around and frowned. "I was sure that I put it with the other things when

I took the tree down last year. But it isn't here, is it?"

After they turned the loft upside down they finally found it, in a shopping bag with wrapping paper and ribbons.

They added the star and placed the gifts beneath the tree. Like a child, Asa picked them up and shook them, guessing the contents of each one.

"Can't we open one?"

"You already talked me into waiting until the day before Christmas to put up the tree," Sarah admonished. "But there'll be no peeking at the presents until tomorrow morning. What would Santa Claus think if there were no gifts under the tree?"

"Santa doesn't need to come, Sarah. I already have everything I'll ever want."

He was so sweet that Sarah couldn't resist. "All right. You can open this one very small package." She pulled out a tiny box, wrapped in red paper and tied with gold ribbon.

"And you open this one." Asa's gift to her was wrapped in green paper with a silver ribbon.

"I want you to know," Sarah said, "that this is the beginning of a tradition that I expect to last for fifty years."

Asa heard a catch in Sarah's voice, happiness welling inside him. He didn't intend to disappoint her. He ripped the paper off and removed the top of the square white box. Inside was a small wooden Christmas ornament. He lifted it out. "A cradle?"

"Yes. Now let me open my gift." Sarah hurriedly pulled the wrappings off and let out a cry of joy. "Bracelets. Silver bracelets." She slid them on one wrist and pressed them against her face. "They're lovely, Asa."

"They're much more than bracelets, Sarah. They're a symbol of what we mean to each other. They're meant to say that you're a treasure more valuable than I can ever say."

"Oh, Asa, that's so lovely. My gift must seem plain in comparison, but it's symbolic, too."

"I don't understand."

"Asa, you've given me a child. I know that we didn't plan to have children, and I know how you feel about sharing me. But nothing in this world will ever come between us. There's enough love in my heart for you and our child. I am so happy. I hope that you'll be happy, too."

"A child? You're going to have our child?" The thought took Asa's breath away. He could only stare at her in wonder. She was right. He'd been afraid to think about bringing a new life into the world. He hadn't been certain that he could stand up to the responsibility. But now that it was happening, he realized it was wonderful.

A child. His and Sarah's child, born of their love. There was a lump in his throat as he tried to speak. "It's fine, Sarah. It will be a new beginning."

He took her arm and touched the bracelets. "Our child will link us forever. And these silver bracelets are a promise to you that my love will never end."

Asa stood up and pulled Sarah to her feet. He added the cradle to the tree, just below the star. Sarah turned off the lights in the room as Asa opened the loft doors wide. Together they watched the beauty of their first Christmas tree send its magic across the barnyard and the pasture beyond.

A church bell pealed.

"It's Christmas Day," Sarah said.

Asa slipped his arms around her, pulling her back against his chest while his hands cupped her stomach. "Merry Christmas, dear Sarah."

The silver bracelets clinked, sending out a soft melody as she placed her hands on his. "Oh, yes," she whispered. "Oh yes."

THE EDITOR'S CORNER

Nothing could possibly put you in more of a carefree, summertime mood than the six LOVESWEPTs we have for you next month. Touching, tender, packed with emotion and wonderfully happy endings, our six upcoming romances are real treasures.

The first of these priceless stories is SARAH'S SIN by Tami Hoag, LOVESWEPT #480, a heart-grabbing tale that throbs with all the ecstasy and uncertainty of forbidden love. When hero Dr. Matt Thorne is injured, he finds himself recuperating in his sister's country inn—with a beautiful, untouched Amish woman as his nurse. Sarah Troyer's innocence and sweetness make the world seem suddenly new for this world-weary Romeo, and he woos her with his masterful bedside manner. The brash ladies' man with the bad-boy grin is Sarah's romantic fantasy come true, but there's a high price to pay for giving herself to one outside the Amish world. You'll cry and cheer for these two memorable characters as they risk everything for love. A marvelous LOVESWEPT from a very gifted author.

From our very own Iris Johansen comes a LOVESWEPT that will drive you wild with excitement—A TOUGH MAN TO TAME, #481. Hero Louis Benoit is a tiger of the financial world, and Mariana Sandell knows the danger of breaching the privacy of his lair to appear before him. Fate has sent her from Sedikhan, the glorious setting of many of Iris's previous books, to seek out Louis and make him a proposition. He's tempted, but more by the mysterious lady herself than her business offer. The secret terror in her eyes arouses his tender, protective instincts, and he vows to move heaven and earth to fend off danger . . . and keep her by his side. This grand love story will leave you breathless. Another keeper from Iris Johansen.

IN THE STILL OF THE NIGHT by Terry Lawrence, LOVESWEPT #482, proves beyond a doubt that nothing could be more romantic than a sultry southern evening. Attorney Brad Lavalier certainly finds it so, especially when he's stealing a hundred steamy kisses from Carolina Palmette. A heartbreaking scandal drove this proud beauty from her Louisiana hometown years before, and now she's back to settle her grandmother's affairs. Though she's stopped believing in the magic of love, working with devilishly sexy Brad awakens a long-denied hunger within her. And only he can slay the dragons of her past and melt her resistance to a searing attraction. Sizzling passion and deep emotion—an unbeatable combination for a marvelous read from Terry Lawrence.

Summer heat is warming you now, but your temperature will rise even higher with ever-popular Fayrene Preston's newest LOVESWEPT, FIRE WITHIN FIRE, #483. Meet powerful businessman Damien Averone, brooding, enigmatic—and burning with need for Ginnie Summers. This alluring woman bewitched him from the moment he saw her on the beach at sunrise, then stoked the flame of his desire with the entrancing music of her guitar on moonlit nights. Only sensual surrender will soothe his fiery ache for the elusive siren. But Ginnie knows the expectations that come with deep attachment, and Damien's demanding intensity is overwhelming. Together these tempestuous lovers create an inferno of passion that will sweep you away. Make sure you have a cool drink handy when you read this one because it is hot, hot, hot!

Please give a big and rousing welcome to brand-new author Cindy Gerard and her first LOVESWEPT—MAVERICK, #484, an explosive novel that will give you a charge. Hero Jesse Kincannon is one dynamite package of rugged masculinity, sex appeal, and renegade ways you can't resist. When he returns to the Flying K Ranch and fixes his smoldering gaze on Amanda Carter, he makes her his own, just as he did years before when she'd been the foreman's young daughter and he was the boss's son. Amanda owns half the ranch now, and Jesse's sudden reappearance is suspicious. However, his outlaw kisses soon convince her that he's after her heart. A riveting romance from one of our New Faces of '91! Don't miss this fabulous new author!

Guaranteed to brighten your day is SHARING SUNRISE by Judy Gill, LOVESWEPT #485. This utterly delightful story features a heroine who's determined to settle down with the only man she has ever wanted . . . except the dashing, virile object of her affection doesn't believe her love has staying power. Marian Crane can't deny that as a youth she was filled with wanderlust, but Rolph McKenzie must realize that now she's ready to commit herself for keeps. This handsome hunk is wary, but he gives her a job as his assistant at the marina—and soon discovers the delicious thrill of her womanly charms. Dare he believe that her eyes glitter not with excitement over faraway places but with promise of forever? You'll relish this delectable treat from Judy Gill.

And be sure to look for our FANFARE novels next month— three thrilling historicals with vastly different settings and times. Ask your bookseller for A LASTING FIRE by the bestselling author of THE MORGAN WOMEN, Beverly Byrne, IN THE SHADOW OF THE MOUNTAIN by the beloved Rosanne Bittner, and THE BONNIE BLUE by LOVESWEPT's own Joan Elliott Pickart.

Happy reading!

With every good wish,

Carolyn Nichols

Carolyn Nichols
Publisher, FANFARE and LOVESWEPT

THE LATEST IN BOOKS
AND AUDIO CASSETTES

Paperbacks

☐	28671	**NOBODY'S FAULT** Nancy Holmes	$5.95
☐	28412	**A SEASON OF SWANS** Celeste De Blasis	$5.95
☐	28354	**SEDUCTION** Amanda Quick	$4.50
☐	28594	**SURRENDER** Amanda Quick	$4.50
☐	28435	**WORLD OF DIFFERENCE** Leonia Blair	$5.95
☐	28416	**RIGHTFULLY MINE** Doris Mortman	$5.95
☐	27032	**FIRST BORN** Doris Mortman	$4.95
☐	27283	**BRAZEN VIRTUE** Nora Roberts	$4.50
☐	27891	**PEOPLE LIKE US** Dominick Dunne	$4.95
☐	27260	**WILD SWAN** Celeste De Blasis	$5.95
☐	25692	**SWAN'S CHANCE** Celeste De Blasis	$5.95
☐	27790	**A WOMAN OF SUBSTANCE** Barbara Taylor Bradford	$5.95

Audio

☐	**SEPTEMBER** by Rosamunde Pilcher Performance by Lynn Redgrave 180 Mins. Double Cassette	45241-X	$15.95
☐	**THE SHELL SEEKERS** by Rosamunde Pilcher Performance by Lynn Redgrave 180 Mins. Double Cassette	48183-9	$14.95
☐	**COLD SASSY TREE** by Olive Ann Burns Performance by Richard Thomas 180 Mins. Double Cassette	45166-9	$14.95
☐	**NOBODY'S FAULT** by Nancy Holmes Performance by Geraldine James 180 Mins. Double Cassette	45250-9	$14.95

60 Minutes to a Better, More Beautiful You!

Now it's easier than ever to awaken your sensuality, stay slim forever—even make yourself irresistible. With Bantam's bestselling subliminal audio tapes, you're only 60 minutes away from a better, more beautiful you!

__ 45004-2	**Slim Forever**	$8.95
__ 45035-2	**Stop Smoking Forever**	$8.95
__ 45022-0	**Positively Change Your Life**	$8.95
__ 45041-7	**Stress Free Forever**	$8.95
__ 45106-5	**Get a Good Night's Sleep**	$7.95
__ 45094-8	**Improve Your Concentration**	$7.95
__ 45172-3	**Develop A Perfect Memory**	$8.95

Bantam Books, Dept. LT, 414 East Golf Road, Des Plaines, IL 60016

Please send me the items I have checked above. I am enclosing $_____ (please add $2.50 to cover postage and handling). Send check or money order, no cash or C.O.D.s please. (Tape offer good in USA only.)

Mr/Ms _____

Address _____

City/State _____ Zip _____

LT-2/91

Please allow four to six weeks for delivery.
Prices and availability subject to change without notice.